For my two sets of double detectives,
　　Alia and Zarena, Zaki and Jaan,
　　Who solved the medical mystery
Of who ate all the cakes in the party bags.

CLUE: Who's got
M otive. And is
U tterly-Opportunistic. And had
M eans to access the kitchen,
(And who had a suspicious sugar rush?)

Sorry, but you shouldn't have left them out,
Think the blame here is fifty-fifty?
Lots of love, Mum xx xx

OXFORD
UNIVERSITY PRESS

Great Clarendon Street, Oxford OX2 6DP

Oxford University Press is a department of the University of Oxford.
It furthers the University's objective of excellence in research, scholarship,
and education by publishing worldwide. Oxford is a registered trade mark of
Oxford University Press in the UK and in certain other countries

British Library Cataloguing in Publication Data
Data available

ISBN: 978-0-19-277359-3

1 3 5 7 9 10 8 6 4 2

Printed in Great Britain

Paper used in the production of this book is a natural,
recyclable product made from wood grown in sustainable forests.
The manufacturing process conforms to the environmental
regulations of the country of origin.

Inside images: Bristol Stool Chart: Cabot Health, Bristol Stool Chart http://cabothealth.com.au/arti-
cles/bristol-stool-chart-2/(accessed 30 November 2013)
Six steps of how to wash your hands: Sandaru Maharamba/Shutterstock.com

A DOUBLE DETECTIVES MEDICAL MYSTERY

THE CURE FOR A CRIME

ROOPA FAROOKI

CHAPTER 1:
HAPPY FAMILIES RHYMES
WITH CHEESE

'So we're doing it? We're really running away, right now?' asked Tulip. She tugged on her school backpack. It was heavy. Too heavy. She dipped her knees, testing it. Looked suspiciously at her twin.

'NOOooo,' said Ali warningly, nodding towards the kitchen, where Mum was carelessly pouring coffee. Really carelessly. Her eyes were sleepwalker blank and she only stopped when the coffee spilled over the table.

Their mum's brand-new boyfriend, Sturgeon, was typing something at the kitchen table, shoulders hunched. He was always working. Being Busy and Important. Since he'd moved in a month ago, he'd taken over their old playroom for his office. He kept it locked like he worked for the secret service. And now he'd spilled over the kitchen table too.

Stupid Sturgeon, thought Tulip. She didn't know why Ali was worried. He never listened to them.

But then he twitched a bit. Just to prove her wrong. And looked up.

'Running?' he said.

'Yeah, but no, but yeah, we're running,' said Ali. 'School running club. Pre-school running club, I mean. And we're late.'

'Gotta go,' agreed Tulip. But she waited at the door, looking expectantly at Mum. Mum just stirred her coffee, and sat down. Flopped down. Her head in her hands like it was too heavy for her neck. '*Bye* then,' Tulip said, insistently. 'See you laters, alligators!'

Sturgeon just jerked his head, and waved his hand, like he was swatting a fly or something.

He didn't smile. He only smiled for photos, when he forced everyone else to smile too. 'Happy Families,' he'd say. Instead of Cheese.

Mum raised her head, but it drooped again. Like the wilted flowers in the jam jar on the table. They'd stolen them from the park for her, when Nan-Nan walked them home. To be more specific, they walked, and she rocked and rolled. In her motorized wheelchair. It had silver go-faster stripes on it and a lightning flash emblazoned on both sides. Nan-Nan was subtle like that.

'Bye, munchkins,' Mum said weakly. It took her another moment, but then she summoned up the energy to say it: 'In a while, crocodiles.'

Ali rolled her eyes, and dragged Tulip down the narrow hallway and out through the front door.

'You know you said that out loud,' complained Ali, as they walked down the street. 'Running away,' she scoffed. 'You'd be a rubbish spy.'

'Not like I'm trying to be a good one,' shrugged Tulip. 'What about you with the Yeah-but-no-but-yeah? Real smooth.'

They'd got to the end of their street. The last house on the corner was the local vets, which had a courtyard for off-street parking and plastic bowls of water for dogs and cats. A cherry tree had spat small hard fruit on the pavement, that were squashed and bruised underfoot.

And the black-witch-cat that always sat there was staring at them from the broken wall. Tulip yanked off her backpack, and dumped it beside the cat. The cat blinked, one green eye, one blue, and then lazily slithered off the loose bricks.

Tulip blinked too. Her lashes were wet.

'What's up?' said Ali.

'Bag's too heavy,' complained Tulip, turning hurriedly away from her. 'What did you put in here, Mum's weights?'

Their mum did twenty minutes of exercise every morning. They used to find it hilarious, watching her bounce around the lounge to school disco tunes. Used to. Now she was just sleepy all the time. She'd stopped exercising in the morning. Stopped doing anything in the morning. Seemed a bit less funny.

'Might've. Thought they'd be good weapons,' said Ali, 'for clubbing stuff when we're out in the wild.'

'What are you planning on clubbing?' said Tulip. 'Rats. Cockroaches . . .'

'Sturgeon,' added Ali, lightly. 'You know, just the usual vermin.'

She watched Tulip blink again. Her big brown eyes reflected two mini-Alis back at her. They were puddle-wide. Puddle-wet. Tulip brushed them with the back of her sleeve.

'What's really up?'

'Mum didn't kiss us goodbye,' said Tulip flatly. She hadn't done that for a few weeks now. She just sat like a zombie-robot at the kitchen table, until she switched herself on to head to work.

Happy Families, thought Tulip scornfully. Right.

Stupid Sturgeon and his stupid teeth which showed too much when he smiled.

Tulip busied herself emptying her backpack.

'Two packs of mini Mars bars?' she asked Ali. 'Two boxes of Pringles? Multi-packs of Haribos?'

'Running away fuel,' explained Ali, promptly. 'All super high-calorie. That means high energy,' she added kindly, as Tulip had raised her eyebrows.

'I know what high-calorie means,' she snapped. 'I mean, what about, I don't know, essentials. Like water?'

Ali sat down on the broken wall with a huff.

'Easy to criticize, isn't it?' she muttered. 'Least I packed. Why don't *you* do some stuff so I can criticize you?'

'Sorry,' said Tulip, sitting next to Ali. She examined the provisions in her schoolbag. 'I like that you got the mini Mars bars. They're yummy melted.'

Ali nodded. Mum wasn't a baker, but she knew what they liked. Their favourite tea-time snack was when Mum melted Mars bars and Rice Krispies together, and put them in fairy cake cases with mini marshmallows. 'Thought we could leave them on a radiator.'

Tulip smiled. 'Must've been hard getting them out of the kitchen,' she said.

'No biggie,' said Ali, 'Stuffed them in my knickers. No one's gonna make me explain chocolate stains in my pants.'

They both cracked up laughing. But then Ali stopped abruptly, she saw two boys crossing the road, walking towards them.

'Zac and Jay,' she hissed. The other twins in their class. The boy twins. Their double nemesis since Year 3. Tulip hurriedly began squashing the packets back in her bag.

'Hey, it's Thing 1 and Thing 2,' said Jay,

the taller of the two boys. He wore specs and thought he was bigger and cleverer than them, but really he was just bigger. By about five finger-widths. Zac, the smaller boy sniggered. But then he smiled apologetically.

'Hey, it's Tweedle-dum and Tweedle-dumber,' said Ali.

'Shouldn't you be at Running Club,' drawled Jay. 'That's where chumps like you get dumped, right?'

This was a sore point with the girls. The pre-school running club involved doing laps around the sports field for half an hour before school. It was where working parents ditched their kids, so they could get to their jobs in time. Kids with a stay-at-home parent could be a bit smug about never having to go.

'Sorry you guys didn't make the cut,' said Ali, 'Heard that running is hard when you're dragging your knuckles on the ground.'

Zac started laughing, but was whacked on the back by his brother.

'Whatevs,' said Jay. 'Our mum stayed home to make us PANCAKES for breakfast. Gluten-free. With organic milk. Just sayin'.'

'Theirs gave them Pringles and Mars bars,'

pointed out Zac. He wasn't saying it like it was a bad thing. He was nodding appreciatively. 'Nice,' he added.

'You can't take that stuff into school,' said Jay. He wiped his glasses like he couldn't believe what he was seeing. 'They're searching bags after the Cola storm.'

The Cola storm was when some kids had smuggled bottles of cheap pound-shop cola into the school, and started a pretty legendary cola-bottle-battle in the corridors. Shaking them up and spraying each other. Coating all the lockers in fizzy brown goop.

'Thanks for the warning,' said Tulip. But Jay and Zac weren't shifting. 'Don't you two have somewhere to be?'

'Same place as you,' said Zac. 'Aren't you coming, Tulip?' He smiled, showing a missing tooth.

'Nope, got the . . .' Tulip improvized wildly, spotting his gappy grin. 'Dentist.'

But Ali said, 'Vet,' at the same time, nodding towards the building behind them.

They looked at each other.

'Dentist-vet,' confirmed Tulip, smoothly. 'Gotta take our cat.' The black-witch-cat had finished licking water out of the bowl. She slithered back to her place on the wall, and sat between them. Licking her paws. There was a damp feather sticking out of her mouth.

'Yeah, she keeps getting bird stuck in her teeth,' said Ali.

'Gross,' said Jay, backing away from the cat, 'We're veggie.' He started shuffling off. 'C'mon, little bro.'

'We're almost exactly the same age,' complained Zac. He followed, but waved at them as he went.

'Ee-yew,' said Ali, rolling her eyes again. 'It's like he doesn't know they're our nemesis.'

'Please, you don't care enough about either of them to be our nemesis,' said Tulip. 'Gluten-free, organic, and veggie. Poor kids. Someone should call child services for them.'

But she gave a small smile to Zac, raising her hand to him, when he turned and gave them a final wave.

'Needy, much?' she added to Ali, like she was excusing herself.

'Come on,' said Ali. 'We're meant to be running away. Let's get going.'

'Which direction?' said Tulip.

'Opposite to where Dumb and Dumber went,' suggested Ali, and they walked up the road towards the station.

Once they were on the train, heading into central London, both girls started feeling a bit funny. Funny-strange, not funny-ha-ha.

'I'm worried about Mum,' said Tulip. 'Not sure we should be leaving her with the Sturgeon.'

'Well, duh,' said Ali, 'that's the point. It's a PROTEST. She can worry about us instead of the other way round.'

'I suppose she'll see she shouldn't have brought Stupid Sturgeon home to play Happy-Families-rhymes-with-Cheese' said Tulip. 'Unless . . .'

'Unless what?' asked Ali sharply.

'Unless she's still too sleepy and tired all the time to work that out. Or even notice. That we're gone.' Tulip shook her head. 'We should go back. Someone's gotta take care of her.'

'Stop guilt-tripping,' said Ali. 'That's *why* we're running away. And you know what? We can keep an eye on her better if we're not at school learning stupid things we already know.'

'What, you mean, just run away to live at the

hospital?' asked Tulip. They hadn't got that far in their planning.

'Works for me,' shrugged Ali. 'Why not?'

'But we can't follow her everywhere in the hospital. People know us. And people will notice.'

Their mum was a junior doctor at a big hospital in town. She hadn't always been one. She used to be a biology teacher at the local academy. It was where she met their dad. He was the chemistry teacher. She said he made awesome illegal fireworks with the school stocks of combustible chemicals.

Their dad looked friendly and fun in photos, but they never really got to know him. He got very ill before they were even in nursery. When their dad died, of something horrible in his brain, Mum decided to go to medical school. She'd started training as a neurosurgeon. She wanted to cut the dodgy bits out of brains.

When the girls were old enough to understand what this meant, it had seemed quite cool.

Unfortunately, that was how Mum had met her boyfriend. Professor Brian Sturgeon. He slimed up to her when she was getting coffee at some Brainiac conference for brain doctors. He described himself as Britain's top brain surgeon.

At the very least. ('I'm the best in Britain, if not the best in Europe, and probably the World!') He said this so often that the girls thought about getting it printed on a T-shirt for him, to save him and everyone else the time.

Mum had always been a bit over-stressed and over-worked, but she'd been fun too. She didn't make illegal fireworks, but she danced badly in lifts and invented the leaning-tower-of-pizza-party-cake and played on the swings with them in the park.

Since Sturgeon had moved in, it was like he'd drained all the fun out of her.

'Nah, nobody'll notice us,' said Ali. 'But maybe don't post it on your Mini-Medix blog.'

'Nobody reads it, anyway,' said Tulip. 'I'm starting a section on infectious diseases. Was gonna call it Twinfectious Diseases.'

'Hah! That's so lame it's almost good,' said Ali.

'Still think we could do with a disguise,' mused Tulip. 'At the hospital.'

'Like what? Shades and a stupid hat like Sturgeon?' scoffed Ali.

'TBH, all hats are stupid,' said Tulip. 'Unless it's hot out and you don't have sunscreen. That's basic sun protection, there's a safe-sun-fun bit on my blog, I called it . . .'

'Twinter is Over,' said Ali. 'I know, I got the link. Sensing a bit of a theme.'

'Aw, you read it!' beamed Tulip. 'I s'pose you're right, the best place to hide is in a crowd,' she mused. 'And hospitals have loos, and telly, and we can get toast in the wards.'

'And water,' added Ali, triumphantly. 'And Wi-Fi! All the essentials. We'll say we're visiting someone we're worried about. Not even a lie.'

The train was pulling into the stop for the hospital.

'Can't believe you read my blog,' grinned Tulip. 'We can work on it together!'

'Great,' said Ali. 'The long twinter nights are just gonna fly by.' She jumped up as the train doors slid open. 'Let's go,' she said, yanking up her heavy bag.

Mum had worked a late shift, which was why she was still at home that morning. Normally she left an hour before them. They used to have the neighbours' teenagers hang out with them as childminders while they ate their cereal, who taught them the best tricks on Minecraft. Shared their Xboxes, too.

Now they just had Sturgeon, who hardly went out to work. He said that since he was already the world's best surgeon he had decided to refocus his interests around research and studies and blue-sky thinking.

It involved a lot of mooching around their house.

Sturgeon knew nothing about Minecraft. He confused Xboxes with eggboxes. He'd chucked their toys out of their old spare-room-playroom and put a lock on it.

Because his stupid studies were so top secret.

Tulip suspected he just watched daytime TV in there. Or napped.

As they stepped off the train, a woman, right behind them, collapsed to the floor.

Ali and Tulip looked around. Everyone else looked somewhere else. Like they were trying hard not to notice the woman on the ground so they could get on with their day.

'Is there a doctor here?' yelled Ali into the swarming crowd.

Nothing.

'A nurse, a paramedic?' yelled Tulip, insistently.

No one answered them. They were just little girls in school uniform.

They were just little girls in school uniform, but they knew what to do.

Ali and Tulip had seen Mum do this lots of times. When Nan-Nan couldn't babysit and Mum was on-call in the night, they'd had to go into the hospital with her. They knew their way around A&E blindfolded. They knew where the secret biscuit drawer was, too.

Tulip ran back towards the lady, and knelt beside her. 'Clear a space,' she yelled crossly to the suits swooping past, to the trainers pattering, and the heels clicking. 'You'll trample her!'

'Can you hear me? What's your name?' bellowed Ali in the lady's ear. She didn't reply. 'Sorry,' said Ali, and she pinched the woman hard between her neck and her shoulders, and the poor floppy woman didn't even try to swat Ali away.

'No response to voice,' said Ali. 'No response to pain.'

'Nooo,' said Tulip, 'That's bad.' She looked around wildly. The crowd had cleared a bit since the train had moved off. She spotted a station manager with a TFL badge.

'Hey you,' she yelled, 'She needs an ambulance.' The station manager nodded, sweating in the heat, and was already on his phone.

And she and Ali counted together 'One, two, three!' and on three, they carefully turned the lady into the recovery position.

'Let's do the ABCs,' said Tulip urgently.

'A! Airway?' said Ali.

'Patent. No blockage,' confirmed Tulip, shining her phone light into the sagging mouth.

'B! Breathing?'

'She's breathing,' nodded Ali, watching the woman's chest rise and fall.

'C! Circulation?'

'I can feel a decent pulse,' said Tulip, holding the lady's hand. 'Maybe there's a clue in her handbag?' She rummaged delicately through it with her fingertips.

'Oh honestly,' said Ali. 'Looking for a lace hanky, your ladyship?' and she grabbed the handbag, yanked it wide open, and dumped the contents so they spilled across the station floor.

'She's diabetic,' Tulip said, spotting the insulin kit among the usual handbag guff and fluff. 'D-E-F-G! Don't Ever Forget Glucose!' She grabbed a tube of sugar gel, and squeezed it into the woman's mouth. The woman's eyes started flickering. She seemed to be coming round. The paramedics came racing down the stairs.

'Think she had a hypo,' Ali said to them. 'We've given her this.' She held up the empty tube.

'Well done, girls,' said the paramedic. 'Is this your mum?' he asked. 'We'll look after her.'

The crowd who'd remained were giving Ali and Tulip a round of applause.

'Um, no,' said Tulip, tidying the things back in the lady's handbag. 'Look, we're just heading off . . .'

'But who are you with?' said the station manager, frowning. 'Are you on your own?'

'Um . . .' They looked desperately around.

And then they heard a familiar electric hum of wheels on the platform.

'Nope, of course they're not on their own,' said Nan-Nan firmly. 'They're with me.'

She was smiling sweetly at the station manager and the paramedics. 'Sorry I was a bit slow. Wheelchair, you know how it is.'

Nan-Nan's smile flicked off like a switch when her eyes fell on the twins. She skewered them with a look of steel.

'Come along, girls,' she said. Her voice was steel too.

Ali and Tulip looked at each other. It was like a silent conversation. They agreed with a subtle head dip that there wasn't anything else they could do. The station manager was still staring at them.

'Yes, Nan-Nan,' they said, meekly.

CHECK PAGE 268 OF THE APPENDIX FOR THE MINI-MEDIX BLOG POST

EMERGENCY TWINTERVENTION!

START WITH ABC

OR WHAT YOU DO WHEN SOMEONE'S COLLAPSED!

CHAPTER 2:
NAN-NAN KNOWS BEST

'How did you know where we were?' asked Tulip, giving Nan-Nan's arm an affectionate squeeze. She was a bit less cross than Ali that their plan had been foiled. Ali gave her a death stare.

'I'll be asking the questions, girls,' snapped Nan-Nan. They got to the steep escalator, and Nan-Nan sighed. 'Why'd you have to pick a station with no lift?'

They had to wait for ages for station staff to help them up the escalator.

'At least it's working,' said Ali brightly, 'There are nine hundred steps in this station.'

This time it was Nan-Nan who gave the death stare.

Nan-Nan's car was parked illegally outside the station with a big disabled sign on it. They called it the Nan-mobile. It had go-faster stripes and a silver lightning flash, just like her wheelchair.

'Well, get in girls,' said Nan-Nan, hauling herself into the driver's seat, and folding her wheelchair expertly with one hand. 'And on the way back to school, you can tell me why you aren't already there.'

The girls sat mutinously in the back. Tulip whispered to Ali, 'Nan-Nan's like a ninja. How'd she even know?'

Nan-Nan was starting the engine, when a cross-looking man started banging on her window.

'Hey you! Parking hog! I needed that space. I've got a cane.'

'I've got a wheelchair,' snapped Nan-Nan to him.

'Cane!'

'Wheelchair beats cane,' she said, rolling her eyes like Ali. 'Evidently.'

'You can just sit in a seat,' he complained. 'Doesn't matter how far away you park. I have to hobble! You can just *roll . . .*'

'You ever rolled off a ramp into traffic?' said Nan-Nan. 'Didn't think so. Because you've got WORKING LEGS.'

There was a silence. And then something strange happened. The cross man laughed. And Nan-Nan laughed. 'You got time for a coffee, Wheels?' the man said.

'Another time, Legs,' said Nan-Nan, passing him a card. 'Got these delinquents to get to school.'

And she pulled off.

The man waved at her. Smiling.

'What happened there?' asked Tulip, confused. Looking back at the man.

'What happened,' said Ali wisely, 'Is that Nan-Nan's got game.'

Nan-Nan wasn't like other grandmas.

Well, maybe, she was just a bit like other grandmas. She was definitely their mum's mum, for a start. That was precisely what 'Nanu' meant in her language, though they'd called her Nan-Nan since they were babies. (She said she was so nice they'd named her twice.) And she was retired from whatever she had done before. And she had a wheelchair, but that was from a 'war wound' (she'd never explained which war) and a 'sporting injury' (she'd never explained which sport, either) and not because she was creaky and decrepit.

But Nan-Nan was not your textbook grandma. She was more a rip-up-the-textbook type. She was more glamorous than their mum, with Hollywood hair that fanned out from her face in waves of black and silver, while Mum's hair was so short it barely needed brushing. She was skinny and strong while their mum was comfortingly cuddly and squishy. She wore jeans and black leather jackets with metal studs, with an extra diamond stud in her nose. Mum wore scrubs or pyjamas or clothes that might as well be scrubs or pyjamas, like leggings and T-shirts. Nan-Nan even smelt glamorous. Like a flower shop. Mum smelt of coffee, biscuits, and soap. And Nan-Nan almost always wore a slash of scarlet lipstick.

But she wasn't today. She noticed that in the mirror, when she stopped at the lights.

'Damn you, munchkins,' she complained to them, 'I went out without my face on. You made me leave in a hurry.'

She flipped open the glove compartment, and

smoothed on her lipstick in one swift movement, an M for the top lip, and the U for the bottom lip.

'How'd you know?' asked Tulip, again. 'Even Mum wouldn't know we weren't at school. They'd text her after register. By then she'd be on the tube.'

Nan-Nan sighed. 'I got them to switch the text alert to my phone, instead of hers. You know your mum's been sort of ... distracted lately. Since she and Brian got back after their weekend away.'

Ali and Tulip looked at each other sharply. Even Nan-Nan had noticed that something was up with Mum. She spotted the look in the rear-view mirror.

'Is that why you skipped school?' she asked. A little sharply. Then, a little softly. 'To get her attention?'

'How'd you find us?' asked Ali, ignoring the question.

Nan-Nan said nothing. Snorted. Like it was a dumb question.

'Silent treatment?' sniffed Ali. 'Seriously?'

'Oh!' said Tulip, 'I know. She's put a tracking app on our phones.'

'Puh-leeze,' said Ali. 'I check our phones for tracking apps. Sturgeon put them on last week, and I deleted them the same day. That's amateur hour.'

'Stupid Sturgeon,' laughed Tulip.

Nan-Nan looked like she wanted to agree. But instead, she took a deep breath, and said, 'Look girls. I know it's hard. But Nan-Nan knows best. I want you both to be much kinder to Brian.'

'Kinder?' asked Tulip, surprised.

'Us . . . ? Kinder . . . to . . . him?' sputtered Ali in disbelief.

'This is going to be a looooong conversation if you keep repeating everything I say,' commented Nan-Nan. 'Yes. Kinder. It can't be easy for him to come into a house with three strong girls.'

'Three?' asked Ali.

'She means Mum,' said Tulip, although she knew what Ali meant. Mum wasn't strong at all these days. Zombie-zoned-out. Since she'd met Sturgeon she was like a different person.

'And it wasn't easy for Minnie being a single, working mum. It's hard to meet new people, when you've got so much on. It was *nice* for her to meet Brian.'

'*Was* nice,' said Tulip. 'For her. For about two minutes. He's no fun to have at home. Even when she's in, it's like she's checked out.'

'And it wasn't nice for us. Not ever,' insisted Ali. 'He's like a big space-occupying lesion in the house.'

'Are you really comparing Brian to a tumour? Or just a pus-filled cyst,' asked Nan-Nan. More amused than cross.

'Nope. You just did,' said Ali. 'Thanks, Nan-Nan,' she added, 'and it's dumb to tell us to be kind to a tumour. Tumours need poisoning with chemo . . .'

'Poisoning?' said Nan-Nan, finally looking alarmed. 'Girls!'

'Oh, relax,' said Ali. 'He never eats with us, anyway.'

'It's not like *you* needed a *Brian*,' pointed out Tulip. 'You were a single mum, and you still managed to do . . . whatever it was you did.' She paused, as she realized she really didn't know. She glanced at her sister, who looked just as clueless.

'Actually, what did you do?' asked Ali. 'I mean, for work.'

'Well, ask a stupid question,' said Nan-Nan. 'I'm a bit insulted.'

'You've never told us,' frowned Tulip.

'Oh, I'm sure I have.'

'Nope,' said Ali.

'Nan-Nan?' asked Tulip. But Nan-Nan remained stubbornly silent.

'And you've still not told us how you tracked us,' pointed out Ali. 'I'm gonna keep asking. And asking and asking . . .'

'Nagging? That's all you've got?' laughed Nan-Nan. 'In my previous career, I was shot at, poisoned, electrocuted, and locked up with biting bugs to make me talk. But nagging? No one ever tried that.'

She ignored their shocked faces. Sometimes it was hard to tell when Nan-Nan was joking.

'Nagging,' she repeated, still laughing, shaking her head. 'Hah! Let me know how that works out for you.' She pulled up at the school. 'Come on, we have to sign in at the front.'

Nan-Nan shrugged off her leather jacket, and pulled on a fluffy cardigan instead. She twisted her thick waves of hair back into a bun, and put on a pair of fake glasses. She transferred neatly into her wheelchair, and pulled a matching fluffy blanket over her skinny jeans.

'You look like the Granny from Little Red Riding Hood,' sniggered Ali.

'Bet *she* didn't keep a pistol in her knickers,' said Nan-Nan. 'I'm getting you out of trouble for this morning. I want gratitude, not attitude.'

'Sure, Nan-Nan,' said Tulip, kicking Ali to stop sniggering.

Nan-Nan rolled into the office, and said sweetly, 'I'm SO sorry I'm late with the girls. I had a bit of trouble with my wheelchair. These little angels helped me. It's so hard being all alone in the world.'

'Of course, of course,' said the school secretary. 'Good work, girls. You won't get marked late. In fact, I'll ask your teacher about extra house points.'

The girls stood gawping at Nan-Nan. 'Give me a kiss, munchkins,' she said sweetly, and then added, in her trademark steel tone, 'and I'm picking you up.' She lowered her voice, 'so don't even think about another unscheduled tourist trip into town.'

Ali wasn't impressed by the menacing tone. 'So, what DID you do, Nan-Nan?'

Nan-Nan shrugged. 'I was a . . . nanny.'

Tulip and Ali looked at each other. They didn't believe that for a moment.

'What, like Mary Poppins?' said Ali, sarcastically.

'Better than,' said Nan-Nan. 'I didn't need magic to clear up other people's mess.'

'But the shooting and electrocuting and poisoning and biting bugs,' persisted Tulip.

'Well, you know what toxic little monsters kids can be,' grinned Nan-Nan. 'Off you go, girls. Spit-spot.'

CHAPTER 3:
THE OTHER TWINS

Ali and Tulip stuffed their bags into their lockers with difficulty. All their illegal snacks were bulking them out.

'Least we missed the bag-check,' said Tulip, squashing the Pringles tube back into the hole at the top of her backpack. She had to give the locker door a karate kick to force it shut.

The bell rang for break, and the other kids began spilling out of the 6X classroom.

'Well, well, well,' said Jay, spotting them. He pushed back his glasses, triumphantly. 'Look who's late.'

'Better late than never,' said Ali. 'For us,

I mean. You can take the never. Don't think anyone would mind.'

'How's the cat, Tulip?' asked Zac, coming out with his arms piled high with books.

'Cat?' she asked.

'Yeah, your cat. She had something up with her teeth,' said Zac. 'Too many birds for breakfast.'

'Oh,' said Tulip, 'she's more our Nan-Nan's cat. We were with Nan-Nan this morning.' She added this bit loudly, as she saw their class teacher coming out.

'I've just heard that, girls,' said Mr Ofu. 'Sounds like we've got two engineers in the class. You really fixed her wheelchair?'

'Well, Google helped,' said Ali, modestly.

Jay wasn't looking convinced. 'What's your cat *called*, Tulip?' he asked.

'Witch,' she lied promptly. 'Why?'

'Well, it's just that there's something trending on YouTube,' he said, pulling out his phone. 'Two kids playing medics on the underground.'

'I sent you the video,' said Zac helpfully, 'Linked it to your Mini-Medix blog.'

'What, you read my blog, too?' said Tulip. 'Aww, Zac.'

'So these kids' faces are pixelated,' persisted

Jay, 'Guess they're not allowed to show them. But check the uniform.'

Ali looked at the screen dismissively. 'Yeah, it would be weirder to see kids who weren't in uniform on a Wednesday morning.'

Tulip glanced at it too. 'Black blazers, black trousers, is that brown or black hair? Flattered, but that could be any pair of kids in the country.'

'Could be *you* guys,' added Ali. 'Where were YOU this morning?'

'We were doing our spelling test,' said Zac promptly. 'I've got next week's spellings for you, Tulip. Oh, and for you, Ali.'

'Thanks, Zac,' said Tulip, taking them off his pile.

'And WE were aiding and abetting the elderly,' huffed Ali. 'Come on, Tulip!'

'You don't even know what abetting means!' Jay called after her.

'Hahaha,' said Tulip, in the girls' toilets. 'I'm gonna tell Nan-Nan you called her elderly.'

'Not if I tell her first,' said Ali. She checked her phone. 'That's quite cool,' she grinned. 'We're seriously trending.'

'Aww, look,' said Tulip, glancing over her

shoulder, 'Zac linked it to my Emergency Twintervention blog post! Hashtag Mini-Medix! We should trademark that for the action figures and the movie.'

'He's spamming your blog?' scoffed Ali, tossing her hair back. 'Kid needs a hobby.' She headed out to the playground, and sat down, staring at her phone.

'Watching the hits go up?' asked Tulip, who'd brought out the spellings with her. She was already making a start on them.

'Trying to work out how Nan-Nan tailed us,' said Ali. 'You're right. She must've installed something on the phone. Not a tracker app. Something hidden, like malware.'

'Paranoid, much,' said Tulip. She started reading through the spellings. 'These are a joke. WAY too easy. Still, sweet of Zac to get them for us.' She paused. 'And way too smart of Jay to work out where we were.'

'Sweet? Smart? The insta-geeks are SPYING on us with social media. You gotta stop playing nice with the enemy,' said Ali. 'You're all, Oh Zac's so sweet, and Jay's so smart. Zac's so kind, Jay's so clever . . .'

'People say the same stuff about us,' said

Tulip, 'One's sweet, the other's smart. One's kind, the other's clever.'

'Who's the *other* one?' said Ali, bristling.

'Well, you're the *other* one,' they both said.

'No, you're *definitely* the other one,' they both repeated, crossly.

Ali crossed her arms in a huff. 'What, you saying you're the sweet one? Saying that no one likes me?'

'Trying not to say that,' pointed out Tulip, 'that's why I'm the kind one.'

Ali didn't reply. It was a sore point with her that Tulip had won the Class Teamwork award last term. It was voted for by their classmates. Which meant it was basically a popularity prize. Tulip had been annoyingly modest about it.

'And it's cool to be the smart one,' said Tulip. 'I'd LOVE to be the smart one.'

'You're just saying that 'cause you think you're smart, too,' said Ali.

'I'll prove you're the smart one,' said Tulip, opening the page of spellings. 'Look, spell "Nosebleed".'

'You're kidding,' said Ali scornfully. 'I'm not going to dignify that with an answer. I'll spell the *medical* for nosebleed. E-P-I-S-T-A-X-I-S.'

'You see,' said Tulip admiringly. 'I don't even know if that's right.'

'It is,' said Jay, from behind them. 'But most people would forget the middle S.'

'Get lost, Insta-geek,' said Ali. 'Didn't ask you over.'

'You kinda did,' said Jay, nodding to the sign on the bench. Ali turned around, appalled at what she saw. She'd unthinkingly sat down on the Buddy Bench. It was where lonely kids sat waiting for a friend to find them when a teacher was too busy to take care of them. It was usually for new Year 3s only.

'Aw,' said Tulip, 'that's nice of you to come over. Maybe you're the sweet one.'

'The what?' said Jay, looking confused.

'We're sitting here *ironically*,' said Ali. 'And where's your sidekick?'

'The little bro's doing something for Mr Ofu,' said Jay, adding with a bit of disgust, 'he volunteered. He's always volunteering for stuff.'

'Wow, that's annoying,' agreed Ali, despite herself.

'I might go and help,' said Tulip, looking across to the classroom.

'Seriously?' said Ali. 'You've already won your class queen prize, give it a rest, already.'

'Can I ask you something?' said Jay, sitting on the bench. 'We've been in the same class since Year 3. We've got stuck with the same dumb double costumes for assemblies since then. The same two-person tasks. It's always been the girl-twins can do this, the boy-twins can do that . . .'

'Is this a question or a monologue?' asked Ali. 'Just trying to plan my breaktime, here.'

'Question is,' said Jay, 'we've got history. Had the same stupid stuff because we were the twins. So why . . .'

'Still not hearing a question,' said Ali, standing up, and dusting off her trousers.

'. . . why don't we get on?' he finally asked.

Ali laughed. 'Well, I like you just fine,' she said. 'Guess I know what you think about me, now,' and she walked off, leaving Jay on the Buddy Bench, looking a bit guilty and bereft.

Tulip chased after Ali, after nodding apologetically at Jay. 'Ali!' she said. 'That was NOT nice. You've made him think that he's the mean one. And you're always saying that he's your nemesis.'

'They're both OUR nemesis,' huffed Ali. 'A little support would be nice.'

'I don't think that's the plural for nemesis,' said Tulip.

'And now you're correcting my grammar,' complained Ali, 'It's like they've infected you.'

'And they're not our enemies,' persisted Tulip. 'Not really. That's just a thing we do. They're just like us, really.'

'No they're not! We're the unique ones,' muttered Ali, rebelliously. 'We're *identical*.'

'Kinda means the opposite of unique,' reasoned Tulip, 'because there's two of us.' In fact, the only way teachers could tell them apart was because Tulip scrupulously cut her hair short, and Ali left hers carelessly long, with a loooong fringe to roll her eyes behind.

Ali was about to retort, when they saw Zac flying towards them in a panic. 'Have you seen my bro,' he said. 'Something's happened.'

Jay had already spotted Zac, and raced over. He turned his back pointedly on Ali, and asked urgently, 'What's up, Zac-Zac?'

'Zac-Zac,' sniggered Ali.

'Shut up,' hissed Tulip. 'We say Nan-Nan for Nanu.'

'Yeah, when we say it, it's cute,' said Ali.

'She said shut up,' said Jay. 'So, what's happened to you?' He looked Zac up and down. Confused. 'You look fine.'

'It's not me,' said Zac impatiently, 'it's Mr Ofu.'

They ran towards the classroom. And there, at his desk, was Mr Ofu. He looked like himself. But not like himself. Holding his head in his hands, like his neck wasn't strong enough to support it. He tried to raise it, when he saw them, and then it drooped down again. The tea he'd poured himself was spilling over the rim of the cup and onto the desk

Ali and Tulip stared at him, and then at each other. They'd seen that before.

They'd seen it that morning. Mum at the kitchen table.

'Alright, kids,' Mr Ofu said, in a strained, hollow voice. 'Sorry about the mess. Think I've had a funny turn.'

'Funny turns are what old people have,' said Ali. 'You're young. Younger than Mum, even.'

'Come to think of it, it wasn't even that funny,' said Mr Ofu. 'Same thing happened last night. My partner found me.'

'What happened?' asked Tulip.

'He said it was like I was asleep,' said Mr Ofu, trying to shrug. But he couldn't even get his shoulders up. 'Lucky there's a doctor in school,' he added. 'Been coming in for some study he's doing. Inspecting old vaccination sites. I was just with him before I came on all strange.'

He nodded, painfully, towards the window that led onto the corridor.

And there, talking to the head teacher, was Brian Sturgeon. He was wearing his stupid hat and shades indoors. Like some celebrity who didn't want to be recognized.

'Sturgeon the Surgeon!' hissed Tulip.

They could hear Sturgeon talking in his irritating, know-it-all tone. 'Oh, I've seen this before. No need to send him home. Or the others. Absolutely not contagious. Know that for a fact.'

Tulip and Ali knew for a fact that something very strange was going on.

'D'you know that guy?' asked Jay.

'He's our mum's . . . boyfriend,' said Tulip, saying the offensive word like pulling off a plaster.

'More like boy-*fiend*,' complained Ali. 'Sleazeball's even moved in.'

'Seriously?' said Zac. 'Never seen him around.'

'He's very new,' said Ali. 'Was kinda hoping he'd just keep going round the revolving door and get spat out the way he came . . .'

'No offence, but what's with the hat and shades?' asked Jay. 'That guy gives me the creeps.'

'Me too,' said Zac. 'No offence,' he repeated.

'None taken,' said Ali. 'Me three.'

For a strange moment, it felt like they were all on the same side.

Tulip didn't say anything. But she reached out for Ali's hand, without really knowing why. It wasn't like she was sad. Or scared.

Ali squeezed her hand back.

'You're right,' said Ali. 'They're not our nemesis.' She jerked her head towards Sturgeon. 'HE is.'

CHAPTER 4:
CATCHING

Mr Ofu managed to get through his next class. But at lunchtime, when all the other teachers raced off to the staffroom with packets of biscuits and their coffee mugs, he stayed in the classroom. He didn't even try to pour himself his usual cup of tea from his flask.

'Sir?' said Tulip, as all the class rattled out of the room like marbles from a tin. But his head was in his hands. He might have been asleep, but he was still sitting.

'It's like he's . . .' Tulip started.

'Powered down,' finished Ali, inspecting him. 'Like Mum.'

Mr Ofu heard them, and raised his head with

an effort. 'Run along, girls,' he said, weakly. He began scratching distractedly at his arm. 'Just need a moment.'

Ali tugged Tulip by the hand. 'Come on,' she said. 'Better do as he says.'

'Aren't you worried about him?' asked Tulip.

'Worried?' said Ali. 'Definitely. I'm worried that whatever he's got might be catching.'

That afternoon was creative writing. They had to write about what they'd do if they were superheroes.

'This is soooo lame,' moaned Ali. 'We've got proper stuff to worry about, and we're stuck wasting our time doing this.'

Jay scoffed. 'Yeah, all the crimes in the city you'd be stopping, if you weren't in class.'

'I know *your* superpower,' retorted Ali. 'Boring for England. Gold medal.'

'I know your superhero name,' he snapped back. 'Ali-Cat, like that mangy carnivorous bird-murdering witch-cat of yours.'

'All cats are carnivorous,' snapped Ali. 'You've heard of the food chain, right? Thought you'd be pleased, at least the birds are *organic*.'

'I've always wanted a cat,' said Tulip dreamily.

'I like drawing them.' She was scribbling pictures around the story she'd written.

'What's your superpower?' asked Zac, who was doodling too.

'I can make people do what I want,' said Tulip, carefully colouring in her cape.

'That seems a little dark for you,' said Zac, surprised.

'No, it's true,' said Tulip. 'I just ask politely. Could you pass me the red pen, when you're done with it, please?'

'Oh, sure,' said Zac. 'Have it now.'

'See,' said Tulip. 'You were using it. And I didn't even need it. Or say why I wanted it.' And she passed it back.

Zac and Jay were open-mouthed at how easily she'd done that.

'You are so much the *other* one,' commented Ali.

'Bet you're glad I'm on your side,' grinned Tulip.

'I'm worried about Mr Ofu,' said Zac. 'He's acting sleepy and weird. Shouldn't we tell someone?'

'Nothing to tell,' said Jay. 'People get sick, sometimes. Not like he's dying.'

Tulip looked sharply at Ali. 'Sick?' She was thinking about Mum. 'We need to talk,' she said urgently to Ali. 'In private.'

Their English teacher, Mrs Khan, came up to their table. She hovered, humming with approval over Jay's work.

'Oh, that's very nice, well DONE,' she said to Jay. 'And such a witty idea, so self-deprecating— the Bore-Boy.' Jay shrugged and tried not to smirk at Ali.

'Here's mine, Mrs Khan,' said Zac.

'Very nice,' repeated Mrs Khan. 'Do tell your mum we loved those South Asian sweets she sent in. They're my favourite. However did she find them?'

'She made them, Miss,' said Zac modestly. 'We helped.'

'Such a talented lady,' sighed Mrs Khan. 'Look forward to seeing her at the Fayre. She's running the tombola again, isn't she?'

Ali mimed being sick. 'Busy, much?' she mouthed. But Tulip knew she was a bit jealous. Their mum had never even done the pick-ups and drop-offs when they were little, and definitely didn't have time to do all the extracurricular school stuff. Ali was convinced that kids with a stay-at-home got more credit from the teachers.

'Oh . . . dear,' said Mrs Khan, looking at Ali's work. 'The Alley-cat? That's a little . . . on the nose, isn't it?'

'Who doesn't like cats?' said Ali casually. Like she didn't care about the approval. 'Not sure you're a progressive enough educator to appreciate my ideas, Miss.'

'Not sure anyone is, dear,' sniffed Mrs Khan. 'So, girls, is your mum volunteering for the Fayre? We could do with a hand for painting the backdrops.'

'Nope, she's working Friday,' said Tulip. 'Brain surgery. She's got a lump to scrape out of someone's head.'

'Well, good for her,' said Mrs Khan, acidly. She rubbed at her arm, distractedly. And Tulip noticed something.

'What's that?' she asked, 'Is that a bruise?'

Mrs Khan looked down at her arm. 'Oh, no, that's just an old injection mark. The BCG, they used to call it. Everyone used to get it . . .'

'It's just a bit . . . blue?' said Tulip. 'Is it always like that?'

'It's really not polite to ask personal questions,' said Mrs Khan. She turned away, calling over her shoulder, 'Ali, work on that at home, please. I'd like to see another paragraph.'

The bell rang before Ali could complain about how unfair it was. 'I wrote the exact same amount as Zac,' she muttered.

'But she barely looked at mine,' said Zac. 'And no one even asked what *my* superhero power was.'

There was a pause. 'So,' said Tulip, 'do you *want* us to ask what your superhero power was . . .'

'Nope,' said Zac. 'Might keep that to myself. I don't take pity questions.' He strolled off.

Ali gathered her books with Tulip. 'You know,' said Tulip, putting away Zac's red pen, 'for a nice kid, he's got a bit of an edge to him.'

'You could say the same thing about you,' said Ali.

They went outside, but Tulip hesitated. She turned to look back at the classroom through the glass panel, watching the last students straggling out and Mrs Khan wandering back to her desk.

'What was it you wanted to talk secretly about, anyway?' asked Ali.

'Maybe there really is something catching,' said Tulip. 'What if Mum's not just sleepy, but sick? And it's spreading! First, Mum, then Mr Ofu, and now . . .' she caught her breath. 'Look!'

When the last student left the class, Mrs Khan sank into her chair, and put her head in the pillow of her arms.

'Doesn't prove anything,' said Ali. 'I mean, she's probably just shattered after a long day of eating home-made sweets.'

'Let's look at Mum's arm,' said Tulip. 'Mr Ofu was scratching his, too. I didn't think anything of it.'

'No, let's finish what we started this morning,' said Ali firmly. 'Let's run away again. And head to Mum's hospital. No one's gonna text Nan-Nan at home time. And stupid Sturgeon won't notice.'

They were just leaving school, when the school secretary ran after them, and caught them at the gate. 'Girls,' she said sharply, 'your walking-home passes have been revoked.'

'What?' said Ali, bristling. 'Why? Who?'

'Sorry, girls,' said the school secretary, 'you'll have to wait for your grown-up.'

'Bet it was Stupid Sturgeon,' muttered Tulip. 'Got bored doing his stupid study.'

But then they heard the familiar hum of a wheelchair. It was Nan-Nan, back in her Granny get-up from Little Red Riding Hood. She'd even sprayed the rest of her hair silver, which Tulip thought was a nice touch.

'Nan-Nan,' said Ali, annoyed and impressed.

'Darn, she's good,' agreed Tulip.

'Going somewhere, girls?' smiled Nan-Nan, sweetly.

CHAPTER 5:
EELS AND SNAILS

'You know, when you say stuff like that, you sound like the scar-faced villain in a 12-rated movie,' commented Tulip.

'12-rated movies?' frowned Nan-Nan. 'Who's letting you watch those?'

'The internet,' said Ali promptly. 'It's our new babysitter since Mum replaced the students with Sturgeon.'

'I'm not saying the villain thing is bad,' added Tulip. 'I'm liking the showmanship. You're ready for panto.'

The other twins approached, with a gaggle of kids from their year. 'That's right, my little cookie-crumbles,' said Nan-Nan, in an over-the-top grandma voice, 'and while Mummy's working, why don't we have a lovely tea party?'

Their frenemies walked by, sniggering behind their hands. 'And we can have some of your little friends over to play, too!' Nan-Nan added mercilessly.

'Yeah, OK, you've made your point,' said Ali, mortified. 'Just stop.'

'You deserve it,' said Nan-Nan. 'Skipping school, sneaking off! And you're lucky no one recognized you doing the Mini-Medix act. I've been working all morning to get that video taken offline.'

They followed Nan-Nan out of the school, but instead of turning towards home, she turned the other way. The road that led towards her place. 'What?' said Ali and Tulip together.

'You think I'm going to leave you two home alone?' said Nan-Nan. 'Brian texted that he's out on research and data-gathering and some such.'

'That what he calls it? Research and data-gathering?' scoffed Ali. 'He was just mooching about school bothering the teachers about their old jabs.'

'I think that's what he said, but I switched

off. Everything the man says turns into blah-blah-blah,' commented Nan-Nan.

Tulip giggled, and Ali looked triumphant, and Nan-Nan realized she might have spoken a bit too frankly. 'I mean, it's nice that he's taking an interest in your school, isn't it?' she added, brightly.

'Nice save,' said Ali. 'Least we know what you really think of him.'

'So he's a bit dull,' shrugged Nan-Nan. 'That's no *crime*, is it?'

She shook out her hair, brushing off the silver spray, and took off the granny glasses. She folded the blanket and the old lady jacket into the pocket of her chair. It turned out that under the fluffy granny clothes, she was in a black tracksuit, with silver stripes like her chair. She was using the exercise model, which she had to wheel with her arms.

'Why is everything you own black or silver?' commented Tulip. 'It's a little OCD, isn't it?'

'Matches my hair,' said Nan-Nan, 'and not everything's black or silver. I flirt with the darker shades of grey.'

'You're like the Bat-Nan,' sniggered Ali.

'Just come home for a bit, and stay there with us?' suggested Tulip.

Ali nodded supportively. It seemed that her idea of getting to the hospital to see Mum was looking less and less likely.

Unless, thought Tulip.

Unless, thought Ali.

Unless they came clean, they thought together.

They had another one of those silent conversations. With Tulip raising her eyebrows, in a *Should-We-Tell-Her* way, and Ali inclining her head and shrugging, in an *I-guess-what've-we-got-to-lose* way.

'Nope, can't do that,' said Nan-Nan. 'I've got my soaps to watch and something exciting in the oven.'

'Look, Nan-Nan,' said Tulip. 'It's really important we go see Mum. We think . . . we think there's something wrong with her. Really wrong.'

Nan-Nan sighed. 'Let's talk about it at home. Spit-spot,' and she wheeled her chair so fast that they had to jog to keep up with her.

Nan-Nan's place was a long walk down the lane, over a bridge and into an industrial estate, backing onto the stuffed cemetery. Nan-Nan's house looked utterly misplaced beside the neighbouring buildings, which were dark, windowless workshops. Nan-Nan had owned the house when the whole area was just little cottages like hers, and open fields. She refused to sell. She said it would be too much effort to move all her stuff. The girls had no idea what she meant by that as her house was hotel-bare. Mum said you could fit all of Nan-Nan's worldly possessions in her personalized carry-on suitcase.

'Doesn't it creep you out living next to all the dead bodies?' asked Tulip, as they went up her drive. Her Nan-mobile was parked outside.

'Nonsense. Corpses are good neighbours,' commented Nan-Nan. 'They don't smoke outside your front door, or steal your parking space, or poke and pry . . . or call the police to break into your place when you're away for a week because there's a rotten smell and flying insects coming from it . . .'

'That last one's a bit specific,' commented Tulip.

'Specific because it's true,' said Nan-Nan. 'They hadn't seen me for a bit so assumed I'd died and gone off.'

'Ee-yew,' said Ali. 'Was it a dead rat or something?'

'Just a curry-in-a-hurry I left out,' said Nan-Nan. 'Had to leave at short notice. When I came home with my roll-on suitcase, they ran away screaming.'

'Because of the curry?' asked Tulip.

'Because they thought I was a ghost,' said Nan-Nan. 'Police forgot to tell them it was a false alarm. Had a nightmare with nosy neighbours when I was in the old country, before I had your mum.'

'Which old country was that again?' asked Ali.

'I forget,' said Nan-Nan, blithely.

'Bit convenient,' commented Tulip.

'Inconvenient,' corrected Nan-Nan. 'Us poor old ladies forget stuff all the time.' She grinned. 'I *might* even forget to tell Mum that you skipped school this morning, if you behave.'

Tulip dumped her bag in the hall, and strolled into the kitchen. She could smell one of Nan-Nan's weird world food experiments cooking in the oven.

'Noooo,' said Ali, saying what they were both thinking. 'She's been looking at *recipes* again.'

'It's eels and snails and garlic, girls,' said Nan-Nan brightly. 'With seaweed foam. And a chilled coulis.'

'Did the three witches from Macbeth lose their cauldron?' asked Ali, sweetly.

'I know you're trying to insult me,' said Nan-Nan, 'but I'm frankly rather impressed you've heard of Macbeth.'

She rolled into the kitchen area, and tapped the stools at the breakfast bar.

'Now . . . sit!' She had her back to them, and pulled stuff out of the freezer and fridge. 'What were you saying about Mum?'

'She's ill,' said Tulip, urgently. 'We think she's been infected . . . by Sturgeon!'

'She's been sick since he's moved in,' added Ali, 'and now he's turning up at school . . . and people are getting sick there, too.'

'Well,' said Nan-Nan, scooping and squirting, and not looking at them at all. 'Prove your hypothesis. If Mum's ill, has she stopped eating?'

The twins looked at each other, shook their heads.

'Fever? Diarrhoea? Vomiting?'

They shook their heads again, feeling a bit foolish.

'She's not herself,' said Tulip, insistently. 'She's tired all the time.'

'All the time? So has she had any days off work?' asked Nan-Nan.

'No,' said Tulip. 'She's still going to the hospital.'

Nan-Nan's silence seemed to say a lot.

'You think we're making it up,' accused Ali. 'That Mum's fine and we just want attention.'

'Oh, there's nothing wrong with wanting your mum's attention,' said Nan-Nan. 'I know all about that.'

She turned her wheelchair around, and her eyes were bright with tears. Real tears. Nan-Nan was always so right and strong. It was crazy to see her like this.

Nan-Nan knew best. She could never be weak. She could never be wrong.

She held up a tray for the twins. And instead of goopy eels and snails with foamy seaweed and slimy coulis, it was a pair of chocolate sundaes. With squirty cream. And sprinkles.

The girls looked at each other. Dessert for dinner? This was much more serious than they thought. This was BAD NEWS.

'You're right, girls,' Nan-Nan said. 'Your Mum's ill. I've known for some time.'

CHAPTER 6:
SENIOR WATER AEROBICS
TRAINING DAY

'What!' said the girls together.

'Well, if you knew,' said Ali, 'why didn't you, I don't know, TELL US!'

'Did you both think you could hide it from us?' said Tulip, 'We're not babies any more.'

'What's she got?' asked Ali. 'Did Sturgeon give it to her?'

Nan-Nan looked a little sad. 'No. Well, yes, in a way. Maybe we all gave it to her,' she said.

'What?' said Tulip.

'I think . . .' said Nan-Nan, 'I think . . . your mum's been under a lot of stress. You know what that means, right? Too much to do and not enough time.'

'Then she should do less stuff,' said Ali promptly.

'And ask for more time to do it in,' added Tulip practically.

'It would be nice if it worked that way,' said Nan-Nan, 'but she's got her job, and it's busy, then she comes home, and she's got you two, and now Brian . . .'

'Stupid Sturgeon,' said Tulip.

'He's like a time thief,' agreed Ali. 'Pus-filled cyst in the spare room.'

'She doesn't say it, but I'll bet she's constantly feeling she's not good enough,' said Nan-Nan, 'because she doesn't get to walk you into school, or do the class bake sale.' Nan-Nan sighed, and finally came out with it. 'Well, I think she's got a bit depressed.'

'Depressed?' said Tulip.

'Because of pick-ups, drop-offs, and bake-offs?' added Ali, not bothering to hide her sarcasm. 'Seriously, Nan-Nan? You've lost it. You're so way off the mark it's like a dot in the distance.'

'Oh, no, Nan-Nan,' said Tulip, much more

kindly. 'That's not what we meant. We meant that she's REALLY ill.'

'Depression IS a real illness,' snapped Nan-Nan. 'Bug-sized bigots. Do you even hear yourselves?'

'We think she's been infected with something by Sturgeon!' said Ali bluntly. 'And now he's doing it to teachers at school, too!'

'What?' said Nan-Nan. She looked properly shocked. Then a bit relieved. Tulip knew what Nan-Nan was thinking. That Sturgeon was something easier to deal with than depression. They could just kick him out to slither back to wherever he'd come from.

'So, girls. You've got my attention,' said Nan-Nan with half a smile. 'Prove your hypothesis.'

After the sundaes had been demolished, and Nan-Nan had finished mopping up her snail-eel-seaweed-mousse with a baguette, she leaned back.

'So your theory is that Professor Brian Sturgeon, a respected neurosurgeon, a few weeks after moving in . . .'

'Oozing in,' interrupted Ali.

'. . . with his girlfriend and her two *adorable*

girls,' carried on Nan-Nan, not bothering to hide her sarcasm either, 'diabolically decides to poison-inject-infect her, delete as appropriate . . .'

'And then does the same to the teachers at school,' nodded Tulip.

'Totes diabolically,' agreed Ali, who was unsure what the word meant but liked the sound of it.

Tulip added urgently to Nan-Nan, 'I'm thinking he's injected their old BCG vaccination site. Using his study as some dodgy excuse. Because it was itchy on Mr Ofu and blue on Mrs Khan!'

'It was!' said Ali. 'If Mum's arm is bruised . . .'

'It'll prove it! Let's go find her!' said Tulip, jumping up. 'Now! Right now!'

'Easy, tigers,' said Nan-Nan. 'I like a good conspiracy theory as much as the next granny. But, just one teeny-weeny question.' She wheeled around and picked up the plastic sundae glasses, dropping them into the dishwasher. 'Why?'

'What?' said Ali.

'What?' said Tulip.

'Not what, cloth-ears,' said Nan-Nan, impatiently. 'Why! Why on earth would he want to make her, or anyone else, sick? What's his *motive*?'

Tulip looked at Ali expectantly, as this was the sort of moment when she would usually say something with a bit of a sarcastic eye-roll, like it was obvious. But then she realized that Ali was looking at her in the same way.

'I'm waiting,' said Nan-Nan, turning to check the oven, where the rest of her snail thing was simmering.

Ali exploded crossly, 'Well, duh, because he's EVIL! He doesn't need a motive. He's like a . . . DISEASE. A big malignant-spreading mum-stealing DISEASE!'

'And people around him are deffo getting sick,' insisted Tulip.

'Yeah!' Ali said. 'It has to be him!'

'Does it?' Nan-Nan raised an eyebrow. 'To be fair, people around *you* are getting sick, too.' She looked at them. 'Maybe you're the ones spreading childish bugs around . . .'

'Us!' said Ali.

'Thanks, Nan-Nan!' complained Tulip.

'Well, I did say that children were toxic little creatures,' said Nan-Nan. 'No offence, girls.'

'Some taken,' huffed Ali.

Nan-Nan was looking at them curiously.

'Depression,' she said. Firmly. Unhappily. 'Sorry girls. It explains a lot.'

'I've got it! Maybe he's such a rubbish doctor, he has to make people sick so he can make them better!' suggested Tulip with a flash of brilliance. '*That's* his motivation! It's a disease. Munchausen by proxy! People make someone else ill, so they get all the attention and credit for looking after them!'

'Interesting. Except that your mum's definitely a non-rubbish doctor,' said Nan-Nan. 'You don't think she'd notice if he was poisoning her coffee?'

'Pretty sure I could poison his and get away with it,' shrugged Ali.

'You could definitely spit in it,' agreed Tulip.

'Girls!' said Nan-Nan.

'Oh relax, Nan-Nan,' Ali said again. 'I told you already, he doesn't even eat with us. He barely eats at all.'

'So he's using her and the teachers like lab rats to see what happens to them,' said Tulip. She felt she was on a bit of a roll. She carried on breathlessly 'Maybe t*hey're* the research and development he's been doing. For some sick Sturgeon bug!' She leaned back triumphantly.

'But, so far, it just makes people sleepy?' said Nan-Nan. 'Not feeling the Nobel Prize here.'

'Well, duh,' said Ali, 'didn't say he was a genius bad guy. Just the bad guy.'

'And what do you know anyway?' said Tulip, frustrated. 'You're no doctor. You were just a . . .'

Nan-Nan's knuckles tightened on the wheels of her chair. She tossed her hair back, and the steam and smoke from her oven billowed dramatically behind her. She turned slowly to face them, looking fierce and furious.

'Just a . . . ?' she asked. With quiet menace. Her voice was like ice.

'Nothing,' said Tulip, just as quietly. Like she was aware she'd gone too far.

'*Nanny*,' said Ali, unrepentantly. 'That's what you said, right? Just Nan-Nan the Nanny.'

'Just Nan-Nan the Nanny,' repeated Nan-Nan. '*Just*. Hah! Well, I think you'll find it was a *very* responsible position.' She finished clearing the sundae and supper clutter. 'I had to leave at a moment's notice. And you won't believe the messes I had to clear up.'

She stuffed her own plastic plates into the dishwasher without rinsing or scraping. It seemed clear that was the end of the conversation.

'So, Brian should be home by now,' she said. 'We might as well go back. If we're lucky we can surprise him in the act of poisoning the local residents.'

Ali rolled her eyes, and jumped from her stool, knocking off the calendar propped on the counter. She picked it up. It incomprehensibly said MIS, in Nan-Nan's curly script. There was no writing on it. Just post-it notes. And the post-it note for that day, had S.W.A.T. written on it. Ali flicked Tulip's arm, showing her the calendar.

'Senior Water Aerobics Training' she mouthed to Tulip.

Tulip frowned. 'You know,' she said, 'I've just realized. We've never been at your place on a Wednesday. You always say that's your senior water aerobics day.'

'What, it's Wednesday!' said Nan-Nan. She stared at her phone in disbelief. 'Girls, why did you have to pick a Wednesday to mess around on!'

'Big deal, so it's Wednesday,' said Ali. 'Sorry you're missing some lame aerobics. You know, you'd think you'd be a bit more WORRIED about your daughter.'

'I've been worried about my daughter for longer than you know!' snapped Nan-Nan, 'Less judging, Judy! Let's get going. We're taking the car . . .'

'Sure, just let me go to the loo . . .' said Tulip, looking around for her bag.

'NO!' exploded Nan-Nan. 'I said we're going. Spit-spot.' She wheeled herself behind them, pushing them ahead of her out of the kitchen and down the wide corridor.

'What if I pee myself?' complained Tulip. 'On your silver and black seat covers.'

'I'll take the risk,' said Nan-Nan, 'And you'll pay for the cleaning bill.' She wheeled right into the back of their legs.

'Ouch! Stop hustling us,' complained Ali.

'Wouldn't have to hustle if you moved your bottoms a bit faster,' Nan-Nan complained back. 'Come on, while we're young!'

'Too late for you,' sniggered Ali.

Nan-Nan's eyes went wide, as she stared at the digital clock over the front door. But as they stared at it too, they realized it wasn't a clock any more. It was a timer.

It was counting down. And it had reached the last ten seconds. 10, 9, 8, 7 . . .

'Nan-Nan, are you OK?' asked Tulip.

4, 3, 2, 1 . . .

And then, a siren began blaring within the house. A red light was flashing around the rooms. And Nan-Nan sighed.

'Too late,' she said. 'They're coming.'

'Who's coming?' asked Ali.

'The senior water aerobics ladies,' said Nan-Nan, too swiftly. 'It's training day, remember.' She pulled back the rug in the hallway. There was a hatch under it, leading to Nan-Nan's basement. They'd never been there. They assumed Nan-Nan had never been there, as basements weren't wheelchair-friendly places. But Nan-Nan pulled up the hatch by the long handle.

Ali and Tulip peered down the hatch. There wasn't a staircase. There was a ramp. It looked helter-skelter steep.

'Well, spit-spot,' said Nan-Nan. 'Get on.' She tapped the back of her wheelchair. The sirens were still blaring. The girls ran to the back of the wheelchair—there were a couple of tiny footrests there. They'd used them like buggy-boards when they were little.

They got on, without another question. Knuckles fighting-tight on the back.

And Nan-Nan slid down the ramp smoothly, and yanked the hatch closed behind them with the hook.

They clung on into the swooping-down-darkness, and heard the sirens stop, with a huge crashing noise, like Nan-Nan's door had just been kicked in.

CHAPTER 7:
SPYiNG ON STURGEON

The girls screamed as they whooshed downhill, the swirling black spinning around them.

'Oh-My-God!' they shrieked, too freaked to even yell Jinx.

'Oh-My-Nan-Nan,' corrected Nan-Nan, as they came to a rough stop, and were flung forward into the basement. They shrieked again, expecting to hit hard wooden floors.

Instead they bounced. And bounced again.

'Hold on,' said Nan-Nan, 'I'll get the lights,' and she clapped her hands, sharply.

A dim light switched on, and they saw they were on a wide floor trampoline. Like the ones in the big flip-out trampoline centre outside of town. Nan-Nan was bouncing beside them, ejected from her wheelchair.

They could hear crashing and smashing upstairs. Had to be several people at least. Sounded more like martial arts fighting than fitness training.

'That was fun,' said Ali, looking back up the steeply curving ramp, 'Can we go again?'

'Wasn't it?' said Nan-Nan, texting briskly. 'But no.'

'You were being sarcastic, right?' said Tulip to Ali.

'I'm not completely sure,' said Ali.

'Training Day?' said Tulip, lying flat on her back. The hatch above them was creaking. 'Huh.'

'Nan-Nan,' said Ali, 'can I ask a question?'

'Of course, munchkin,' said Nan-Nan. She was commando-crawling expertly towards her upturned wheelchair, which was bouncing gently near the edge of the trampoline.

'What's happening?' sputtered Ali. 'I mean, what's going on up there? And what IS this place?' She gestured wildly around, at the trampoline and the dark walls.

Nan-Nan hauled her wheelchair over to the edge of the trampoline, and let it drop to the floor, where it fell neatly on the wheels.

'Well, that was more than one question,' she pointed out. 'Thought you girls had mastered counting by now . . .'

'Nan-Nan,' said Ali warningly, in a cross voice.

'Nan-Nan,' said Tulip, in a small voice, 'I'm a bit scared.'

'Oh sweetie,' said Nan-Nan, putting her strong arms around Tulip. 'There's nothing to be scared about!' She nodded towards the ceiling. 'It's just the senior water aerobics girls. My team. We have our training day on Wednesdays. They come to me because of the . . . wheelchair. And this place,' she said blandly, 'it's my basement. Obviously.'

'Looks more like a panic room,' said Ali, 'Why are you hiding here?'

'*She's* not hiding,' said Tulip, pulling back from Nan-Nan. 'She's hiding us.' She looked wide-eyed at Nan-Nan. 'She doesn't want us to meet her . . . team.'

'Of course I don't,' said Nan-Nan. 'You two are pretty embarrassing. No offence.'

'And that's why you dragged us down here and wouldn't even let me pee?' said Tulip.

'Can you think of a better reason?' said Nan-Nan.

She had them there.

'Yeah,' said Tulip doubtfully. 'I guess that's almost credible. But wouldn't you need water, though? For water aerobics.'

'So much harder to swim on dry land,' said Nan-Nan, promptly. 'You try it.'

'How long are they going to . . . train for?' asked Ali. Playing along. Looking warily at the creaking ceiling.

'Oh, long enough for us to watch something on the telly,' said Nan-Nan. 'I've got a rec room down here.' She slid into her wheelchair, and rolled through a metal door at the side of the room, tapping a coded panel.

They looked around the rec room, which seemed more like a regular living room than the one upstairs. There was a squashy sofa with cushions, and a board plastered with photos of their mum as a baby with Nan-Nan, who seemed to be dressed up in lots of different national costumes. In one she was wearing a jewel-coloured sari. In another, a stiff-looking orange patterned cloth, with a matching pleated headdress covering her hair. In yet another, she was all in black robes, with her hair and mouth covered, so just her gleaming eyes were showing. In another, she was in a checked shirt and jeans, with a scarf and a cowboy hat. Mum just looked the same in all of the shots—a little baby-blob in marshmallow outfits, with a brown fluff of sticky-up hair. Waving fat fists with her camera-face fixed on, screwed-up eyes and a wide gappy mouth squealing 'eeeeeeee!'

'Was this a parade, or something?' asked Ali, confused. 'Or model United Nations? You're India, Africa, the Middle East . . .'

'And the Americas,' said Tulip. 'Check the cowboy hat.'

'What?' said Nan-Nan, and she started hurriedly taking down the photos. 'Yes, something like that, munchkins,' she said. 'The cowboy hat was so much easier to get hold of than the cow.' She flicked on the TV, and began clearing the papers on the low table. They had a MIS written on them too, in her curly writing.

'You're missing an S in MISS,' commented Tulip. Nan-Nan wasn't a MRS as she'd never married. She made a point of it anytime someone got it wrong.

'So, what do you want to watch?' she said.

'I've got Netflix. Pretend you're on a plane, pick any movie you want.'

'Never been on a plane,' commented Ali. 'Don't even have a passport.'

'Borrow one of Nan-Nan's,' said Tulip, watching Nan-Nan put away several of the little booklets. 'Are those all your expired ones?'

'Oh, yes,' said Nan-Nan. 'Expired, definitely.'

'Thought you only needed a new one every ten years,' said Ali. 'That's what Mum said. You've gotta have a dozen, there.'

'Well, you don't know how old I am,' said Nan-Nan. 'And I moved around a lot. In my job. As a . . .'

'Yeah, yeah,' said Ali, 'as a nanny. An international-leave-your-curry-in-a-hurry-mess-cleaning-nanny.'

'Dealing with nanny-ing emergencies around the world,' added Tulip. She looked about the room, the tables were littered with strange tech. 'Why have we never been down here?'

'The ramp,' said Nan-Nan. 'It's made for a wheelchair, not for feet.'

'Huh,' said Ali. 'And what are those?' She was pointing at a glass cabinet, with strange metal sculptures. Pointy and vicious-looking.

There were two of them, mirror-image identical.

'Artist's impression of you, when you were babies,' said Nan-Nan. She flicked channels on the TV. And for a moment, there was a split screen of long wooden tables with official-looking types in suits, having a meeting. The word MIS again. Except the top of the S looked straighter. Nan-Nan hastily flicked to a kids' channel.

'Oh, Blue Peter,' she said brightly. 'Love that. Your Mum got her first Blue Peter badge when she was eight. You're falling behind, girls.'

'It's almost like you're appealing to my competitive side to change the subject,' said Ali. She looked at Tulip, who nodded.

'Nan-Nan,' said Tulip, carefully. 'There's something mad going on upstairs. You've got an emergency escape ramp downstairs. A basement that basically looks like the batcave. And that screen either said MI5 or I need specs . . .'

Nan-Nan sighed. 'You *had* to do this on a Wednesday,' she muttered. Unrepentantly. 'I keep telling you, that's Me-time, not We-time . . .'

'With the water aerobics team, yeah, yeah,' said Ali.

'And those aren't sculptures of us,' said Tulip. 'Those are blades, right? They look like, I dunno, weapons or something. Why're they locked up?'

'They're not in use. Look,' said Nan-Nan. 'This is a long story, and there's no easy way to say this . . .'

'So. Were you a spy?' asked Ali. Bluntly.

Nan-Nan scoffed and said nothing.

'Oh. You *were* a spy,' said Tulip. Firmly.

'Stand corrected,' said Nan-Nan. 'Turns out there *was* an easy way to say it. But it's still a loooong story, which I don't have the time or inclination to tell.'

'Of course you wouldn't tell us!' exploded Ali. 'You don't tell us about Mum, you don't tell us about you. You never tell us ANYTHING!'

'One word,' snapped Nan-Nan. 'Deniability.'

'Don't know what that means,' complained Tulip.

'Well, look it up, sweetheart,' said Nan-Nan.

Ali had been pacing around in front of the console. 'It means, if anyone asked us about Nan-Nan, we wouldn't know enough to say anything.'

'Nan-Nan,' said Tulip crossly, 'I thought you

were nice. Nice grandmothers DO NOT lie to their grandchildren.'

'Of course I'm not nice,' said Nan-Nan, appalled. 'That's an ugly accusation.'

'Does Mum even know?' asked Ali.

Nan-Nan shrugged. 'Your mum was a baby when I was active. She couldn't even poo in a potty. She definitely didn't ask annoying questions.'

'You don't look like a spy,' commented Ali.

'Well, that's sort of the point,' said Nan-Nan, 'And when I lost my legs, I couldn't do, so I taught. Spy-trainers are just like nannies, we look after the newbies in the firm. So it wasn't the biggest lie.'

'Spy-trainer,' repeated Ali. She turned to Tulip. 'I guess that's kind of cool.'

'NO! Not cool,' said Tulip, stubbornly. She looked accusingly at Nan-Nan. 'I still don't get why you're not worried about what Sneaky Sturgeon's up to.'

'Because,' said Nan-Nan, 'I know EXACTLY what he's up to!'

'What!' said Ali and Tulip together. 'Jinx,' they said. 'Jinx, padlock, 1-2-3 . . .'

'Really?' said Nan-Nan. 'You two still do that?'

'What's he up to?' said Ali.

'And how do you know?' said Tulip.

'You two are like mosquitos,' complained Nan-Nan, 'You're just pick-pick-pick.' She picked up the remote, and channel-hopped on the TV again. The image flickered to another set of split screens. Like security camera views in a high street shop. But disconcertingly familiar.

'Hold on,' said Ali, 'is that . . . our house?'

'Kitchen, hall, front garden, playroom, everything,' said Nan-Nan. 'Sometimes I had to run off at short notice when I was babysitting. Seemed like a good idea.'

'Nan-Nan!' exploded Tulip. 'That is not nice and not legal!'

'Don't worry, I didn't do the bathroom,' said Nan-Nan. 'No one saw you poo on a loo-cam. Too many forms to fill in for that one.'

'You left us home-alone? But what if . . . someone came to the door! And checked!' said Ali.

'Oh, I can divert the doorbell, too,' said Nan-Nan. 'Watch this,' as a postman was walking up the front path with a big package.

She activated an app, and when the postman

pressed the doorbell, it was Nan-Nan's phone that chimed with the familiar ding-dong. 'Hello?' she said.

'Delivery,' chirped the man, to the intercom.

'Oh, shoot, I've just done my nails, dear. Could you leave it behind the rosemary bush?'

'No problem, Madam,' said the delivery man. 'But it needs signing for?'

'Just do a smiley face,' said Nan-Nan. 'I'd do it myself, but I'm not messing up my manicure. Got a hot date . . .'

The delivery man laughed, and dropped the package behind the bush. 'Good luck!'

'Oh, I don't need luck,' said Nan-Nan. She flicked off the intercom, and winked at the girls. 'Good tech beats good luck.'

Ali and Tulip were open-mouthed. 'Can I do that next time!' Ali said excitedly. 'Can I order take-out and get someone else to come to the door!'

'No, you cannot,' said Nan-Nan.

Tulip walked up to the split screens, and pointed to one particular view. Their old playroom. Sturgeon's table and bed, littered with papers. The chair where he sat.

'You were lying, Nan-Nan,' she said. 'You

said you WERE a spy. But that's wrong, you ARE a spy.'

Ali nodded. 'You've been spying on Sturgeon!' she said triumphantly.

CHAPTER 8:
CREEPY DOLL

'Well, I'm not proud of myself,' said Nan-Nan. 'I always promised not to interfere in Minnie's love life. But ... well ...'

'Well, that PROVES it,' said Tulip. 'You're suspicious of Sturgeon, too.'

'Hah,' said Ali, fist-bumping Tulip and pulling back with a finger wave. 'Knew it!'

'Well, Minnie's never been the brightest with boyfriends,' said Nan-Nan, defensively. 'You should've seen the knuckle-draggers she had hanging round her at school. And this whirlwind romance with ... well, *Him* ... it took me by surprise.'

'Don't know what she sees in him,' agreed Ali. 'Love at first fright.'

'Actually, I didn't get what he saw in her,' said Nan-Nan.

'What!' exploded Ali.

'She's worth a million of him!' Tulip huffed.

'Well, technically, he's worth a million of her,' commented Nan-Nan. 'He's a top neurosurgeon. He's ridiculously wealthy with a massive mansion in the country . . .'

'Sounds like YOU want to marry him,' sniggered Ali.

'Yeah, Sturgeon's a catch!' laughed Tulip. 'Geddit! He's a Dishy Fishy!'

Nan-Nan frowned them down and carried on. 'And yet he's chosen to move into a tiny terrace with a woman who's got two snarling wolverines for children . . . No offence, girls.'

'Some taken,' huffed Ali, again.

Nan-Nan's phone buzzed. She checked it, and grinned like she'd got good news. 'Back in a moment, girls,' she said, putting it next to the remote. 'Don't touch anything. I haven't found the self-destruct button for the basement in days, and can't remember if I left it plugged in.' She wheeled out smoothly.

'She was joking about that, right?' said Tulip.

'Seriously, who can tell any more?' said Ali. She googled Sturgeon on Wikipedia. 'Nan-Nan's right. He's so rich it's ridic.'

'Check the photo,' said Tulip. It was a black-and-white newspaper shot of Sturgeon as a teenager. Winning some student prize. 'How big is his hair!'

'Hair-larious! Wouldn't know it was him,' commented Ali.

But then Tulip pointed to the screens. Someone was stalking up to their front door. In a familiar stupid hat and shades.

'Ugh, he's back!' said Tulip.

But then Sturgeon did something weird. He looked shiftily up and down the street. And instead of fiddling for his keys, to open the door, he pressed the bell.

The smart-intercom rang on Nan-Nan's phone. Tulip's hand hovered towards it, automatically.

'Don't *answer* it!' hissed Ali, slapping Tulip's hand away.

He rang again.

'Doesn't he know that he's not in?' said Tulip. 'Stupid Sturgeon.'

'He's checking that *we're* not in,' said Ali.

'What's he doing that's so top secret?' asked Tulip.

They watched Sturgeon take out his keys, apparently satisfied, and he gave another quick look along the road. No one was there. Except the black witch-cat, who had jumped on the low wall they shared with their neighbour. Staring at him.

'Shoo,' he said, swatting at the cat. She arched her back and hissed, turning briefly from self-satisfied vagrant into furious-furred monster.

'I've always liked that cat,' said Ali.

'Go! GO!' complained Sturgeon, he lifted his foot, as though ready to kick the cat off the wall.

Witch didn't like that. She leapt at Sturgeon, biting at his pockets, swiping viciously at them. He helplessly flailed around in circles. It was like Witch had eight sets of paws and claws.

'We totally should adopt her,' cracked up Tulip. 'I'm gonna get me some popcorn and enjoy the show.'

'Do you think there's something FISHY in Sturgeon's pockets,' joked Ali, slapping the counter while she laughed.

'Not such a CATCH now, are you, Sturgeon?'

carried on Tulip, as his shades went askew and his stupid hat got mauled and dragged halfway off.

'Actually, what HAS he got in his pockets?' said Ali, peering closer at the monitor. 'The cat's super-keen on it.'

Something had tumbled out of Sturgeon's pocket. Smaller than a pen, larger than a battery. They couldn't really see what it was. Sturgeon grabbed it, and tossed the cat over the wall into the next-door neighbour's garden. He pushed his key in and tumbled almost drunkenly into the house, slamming the door behind him.

They watched Sturgeon stride straight upstairs, and then into their old playroom, and slam that door behind him too. The camera switched to a view of the desk. He slumped at it, and only then did he pull off his shades and hat.

'Where do you think the cameras are?' asked Ali. 'You'd think we'd have noticed them. Nan-Nan's got our place more bugged than an ant farm.'

'The camera must be in the bit of the room we can't see,' mused Tulip. 'There's that shelf next to the window. With Mum's old toys on it.'

'Mum's toys!' said Ali. 'They're all over the

house. Oldie-Worldy-Ancient-Teddy-Button-Eyed crud. Didn't think anything of it.'

'And those creepy glass-eyed dolls! Nan-Nan always told us not to touch them, because they're too fragile!' said Tulip.

'Like we ever would,' said Ali. 'The only thing I'd do with those dolls is bury them in a deep dark place.'

'Bigger picture,' said Tulip, 'violation of our privacy. Nan-Nan could edit together a whole reality-show of us.'

'Oh relax,' said Ali. 'It's not like she's posting our hilarious conversations on her Insta-gran feed.'

'And if she did, I'd want all rights,' said Tulip. 'And I'd like the poster to be us standing back-to-back holding syringes. Maybe a stethoscope, too.'

'You see,' said Nan-Nan, rolling into the room, glancing dismissively at Sturgeon slumped on the screen. 'He doesn't do anything at all.'

'Awesome tech,' said Ali. 'I'm promoting you to our Sensei.'

'I'm your Sensei?' said Nan-Nan, looking briefly pleased. 'What's a Sensei?'

'A mentor, who looks like a weak old person, usually with a big beard, like Master Wu or

Gandalf, or small and wrinkly like Yoda . . .'

'I'm getting less and less flattered,' said Nan-Nan.

'But who's really a fierce warrior with hidden depths.'

'Better,' said Nan-Nan.

The noise upstairs had disappeared. Tulip supposed that Nan-Nan's guests had finished their training. 'Come on, girls,' said Nan-Nan. 'Let's go out the back door.'

'Back door?' said Tulip. 'I thought the whole point of basements is that they're single-point-of-entry traps.'

'Where they push you downstairs and unleash the beast,' agreed Ali. 'It's like the horror movies have been lying to us.'

'Remind me to sort the parental controls on your streaming,' said Nan-Nan. 'Of course there's a back door. How would I roll up that ramp?'

Tulip turned back to the monitors. Their mum was coming up the path, with a bag of doughnuts.

'Hey, look, Mum bought dessert for dinner too,' said Ali.

Mum tiredly petted the witch-cat, who licked her fingers. Picked up the package behind the bush that Stupid Sturgeon had ignored, and balancing it awkwardly, went into the house.

'Spit-spot,' said Nan-Nan, wheeling off. The girls followed her to the end of the basement, where there was a door that was almost invisible. It was flush with the wall and painted black.

'How d'you open it?' asked Ali.

'Motion-sensor,' said Nan-Nan. 'Very high-tech.' Then she punched the door with an impressive karate chop, and the lock gave way.

'Nice move, Sensei,' said Tulip.

'I know,' said Nan-Nan, smugly. 'Don't need *your* approval to feel all warm and fluffy about myself.'

She rolled through the door, and they went down a damp, cement-lined tunnel. It terminated at a little round opening, concealed by the bushes and closed with a rusty grate and an old-fashioned padlock.

They took the shortcut home along the field, picking yellow flowers for Mum, to replace the dying weeds on the kitchen table. They were home as the sun was setting, and the sky was marmalade with beetroot. Like one of Mum's random sandwiches when they'd forgotten to do the shopping.

'I'm leaving you here,' said Nan-Nan, at the front door. 'Kiss your mum for me. I'm late for a date.'

A car was pulling up on the other side of the road. 'Hey, Wheels!' called the cross man from that morning. He looked a lot less cross. He was waving and carrying a massive bunch of flowers.

'Hey, Legs,' said Nan-Nan. 'Be over in a moment,' and she kissed them firmly, and shooed them into the house.

'Is that you, munchkins?' called out Mum, wearily, as they stepped into the hall, stamping mud from their shoes.

'It's us,' Ali confirmed. 'Nan-Nan brought us home. We were late because of . . . her water aerobics.'

'That's no excuse,' said Sturgeon crisply, emerging from the spare room. He looked down the stairs and down his nose at them. 'Hope your grandmother fed you. There's nothing but hard cheese in the fridge. Now put yourselves to bed. Your mother's very tired.'

He blinked his eyes, as Tulip took a shot of him on her phone while he was still finger wagging.

'Happy Families,' chanted Tulip. He harrumphed and went back into the spare room, slamming the door behind him.

Ali looked up at the creepy glass-eyed doll in the hallway, high on the shelf, and rolled her eyes at it.

'Rhymes with hard cheese,' she said. She was sure Nan-Nan was still watching them.

CHAPTER 9:
SLEEPY SCHOOL

The next morning the twins fixed their own breakfast, again. Sturgeon was locked in his super-secret room. Mum was still in bed. Tulip dutifully microwaved porridge and doled it out for the two of them.

'Thanks,' said Ali, staring at her phone. She tossed grapes in her mouth, missing half the time. They rolled on the floor, and Tulip narrowly avoided squishing them in her socks as she walked.

'You're welcome, munchkin,' said Tulip. 'Now eat nicely. And you're picking those up.' She kicked a grape towards Ali.

'OMG,' cried out Ali. 'Are you trying to be MUM?'

'Nooo,' said Tulip, hurriedly. 'I was saying that ironically. Obvs.'

Ali didn't look convinced.

'Oh, maybe I was,' admitted Tulip. She pulled off Mum's apron, and chucked it on the back of a chair. 'Feels like someone has to be. There's kind of a vacancy . . .'

'Yeah, like the one in Sturgeon's head,' scoffed Ali.

'And Nan-Nan told us to be *nicer* to him,' said Tulip.

'Well Nan-Nan can just . . . roll off,' said Ali. 'She's not the boss of us. And she's not even here.' She rebelliously chucked her porridge into the food waste bin. And got out a cookie packet, and began breaking them into her cereal bowl instead.

'Cookies? For breakfast?' said Tulip. Half in shock. Half in awe.

'And tomorrow, I'm microwaving pizza,' said Ali. 'There's no prize for eating porridge if no one's even watching us. And telling us we're good.'

'I like porridge,' said Tulip, dreamily. 'I like how it's warm and creamy. It's the opposite of ice cream, but in a nice way.' She squirted honey over it in pretty swirls.

Ali chewed her cookies with difficulty. But determination.

'Are those alright?' asked Tulip, pouring more porridge down her throat.

'They're sort of dry,' admitted Ali. She poured some milk over them. And then they quickly turned into a depressing grey mush with black bits that were the chocolate chips.

Ali stared at the mush. Tulip stared at the mush.

Ali took a spoon, and ate it. Stubbornly.

'Better?' asked Tulip, trying not to laugh.

'Much,' lied Ali. She pushed her bowl away. 'Let's go talk to Mum.'

Tulip scooped the rest of her porridge into her mouth, and followed Ali up the stairs. They could hear Sturgeon tapping on his keyboard in his room.

'Leave your mother alone,' he called out to them, as they crossed on the landing. 'She needs her sleep.'

'We're just going to pee,' called Tulip.

'You can pee downstairs,' he called back.

'And we have to talk to Mum about . . . the school Fayre,' Tulip added.

'No, you don't,' he yelled.

'No, we don't,' agreed Ali. 'That was a lie. We *actually* have to talk to Mum about girl stuff.'

There was silence.

'Girl stuff?' he said.

'Girl stuff?' mouthed Tulip, looking questioningly at Ali.

'I don't want to get into the details,' said Ali. 'But we're not talking pink flying unicorns.'

It worked like magic. Sturgeon shut up altogether.

'I've gotta remember that phrase,' whispered Tulip, as they climbed the rest of the stairs. 'Girl stuff?'

'It's how Layla always gets out of gym,' Ali whispered back. 'Teachers really don't want to have any conversation ever about girl stuff. They just go all silent and embarrassed.'

They gently pushed open their mother's door. She was sound asleep. Tulip snuggled next to her, and gave her a big hug, 'Mama-bear,' she said. 'We're off to school in a moment.'

'Love you munchkins,' she murmured. Still half asleep. 'See you laters, alligat . . .' She couldn't even finish the word. It was awful.

'Are you alright, Mum?' asked Ali. She gave Mum an even bigger hug. And then let go suddenly. Like she didn't want to seem too needy. 'We were wondering if you were sick.'

'Yeah, no, I'm fine, munchkins,' said Mum. 'Sorry, I meant to make you breakfast, I really did, but I'm just so, so . . .'

'Sleepy?' said Tulip.

Mum could only yawn for an answer.

'Mama-bear,' persisted Tulip, 'there's the school Fayre tomorrow. Mrs Khan was asking . . . well, I know you're working, but . . .'

'School Fayre?' said Mum, suddenly stirring. 'I'll be there.'

'What?' said Ali. 'Thought you're doing an operation . . .'

'I'll be there,' murmured Mum. 'I think I definitely have to be,' before nodding off again.

'Mum,' said Tulip, 'I really don't think you should be going to work like this . . .'

'Don't worry, darlings. Brian'll wake me up,' said Mum. 'He always does . . .'

She was gone. Breathing deeply. With a slight snuffly snore.

'I don't like this,' said Tulip. 'It's getting worse.'

Ali pulled back the covers, and they inspected

Mum's arm. There really was a bruise over the BCG mark. And a bobbly rash.

'X marks the spot,' said Tulip, looking at Ali. She couldn't quite believe they'd been right.

The package that Mum had collected was in the corner of the bedroom. It was addressed to both her and Sturgeon.

'Moving-in present?' suggested Ali. She picked it up, and shook it. Experimentally. 'Stupid-boyfriend-stupid-Sturgeon,' she said, shaking it harder. There was the tinkling snap of glass breaking.

'That doesn't sound good,' said Tulip.

Ali looked briefly panicked. 'How was I meant to know?' she complained. 'Who posts glass?'

Tulip calmly picked up the box, and put it outside the spare room door. 'Let's finish breakfast.'

They tidied away their bowls hurriedly, in case Sturgeon came down for breakfast. They never saw him eat, but he bought loads of mushrooms. The fridge was full of them. They seemed to be multiplying in there.

'There's not much room, with the mushrooms,' said Tulip, as she tried to find a place for the milk. She had to juggle the cheese and margarine.

'That was awful,' said Ali bluntly. 'Next time say stuff like that in your head before you say it out loud.'

''Cause Sturgeon's such a *fun-guy*,' said Tulip, shrugging on her coat. 'Come on? Fun-gi!'

'That's even worse,' said Ali. 'You're like last year's Christmas cracker.'

'We're off now,' Tulip yelled from the front door. They heard Sturgeon leave his room immediately, like he'd been waiting for them to go. They heard the smash and crash as he stepped onto the package. 'Oh, and we found a delivery, we left it outside your door,' she added, helpfully.

They walked briskly down the front path. 'Now it's his fault it broke, not yours,' said Tulip practically.

'You're right,' said Ali. 'I'm glad you're on my side.'

When they were almost at the vet's at the end of the street, Ali switched off her phone, and pulled out the battery. 'Give me yours!' she said. 'Nan-Nan can't tail us.'

'Mine's in my bag, at Nan-Nan's,' said Tulip. 'What, are we running away again? Why didn't you say?'

'Nan-Nan's got the place bugged,' said Ali. 'Duh.'

Witch-cat was waiting for them. She leapt off the wall, with fresh feathers in her mouth, and slithered around Ali's legs.

'Mangy alley-cat thinks we're friends now,' moaned Ali.

'Aww, she's an *Ali*-cat,' said Tulip.

A car pulled up. With Jay and Zac in the back. Jay was waving smugly. Zac was just waving.

'You can drop us off here, Dad,' said Zac. 'We'll walk with Ali and Tulip.'

'Hello girls,' said their dad. 'Bumped into your grandmother. She was on the way over with your schoolbags.'

'Oh, thanks, Mr . . .' said Ali, holding out her hand for it.

'Oh, none of this Mister nonsense,' he interrupted. 'Call me Wiggie.' He opened the doors. 'Hop in girls, I'll give you a ride to school.'

'Oh,' said Tulip. 'That's really kind. But we're just on our way to . . .'

'Hospital,' said Ali. 'We've got an appointment. Guess Nan-Nan forgot. Silly old forgetful Nan-Nan.'

'Oh, no, she didn't forget,' said Wiggie. 'She

specifically told me to tell you that whatever-it-was you said you had to do at the hospital had been cancelled. And you were to go straight to school. Spit-spot.'

'That sounds just like her,' said Tulip.

'Darn, she's good,' said Ali. 'She doesn't even roll up in person. She just sends in her minions now.'

'Minions?' asked Wiggie, looking around. 'Where?'

'Really, we're fine to walk,' said Tulip.

'Oh, it's no trouble,' said Wiggie. 'Boys, scooch up for your friends.'

The girls sighed. It was hard to argue with such persistent niceness. Ali took the front seat, and Tulip squashed into the back with the boys.

'So I'm the tallest,' complained Jay, 'and I'm in the middle in the back.'

'Someone sounds cranky,' said his dad indulgently. 'Here, have an organic nut-and-fruit bar. It's got no-added-sugar,' he nodded to Ali.

'Yum, No-added-sugar. That's my favourite ingredient,' said Ali, with a perfectly straight face. 'So, Wiggie? That's an . . .'

'. . . *unusual* name,' said Tulip. Warningly. She mouthed, 'Be nice!' in the rear-view mirror. At least Wiggie couldn't possibly be wearing a wig. He was hairless. He'd either shaved his head or was completely bald.

'You wouldn't believe the trouble I had with it at school,' Wiggie laughed. 'I had big hair, back then. Like a disco afro.'

'Kids can be cruel,' said Tulip. Zac nodded. Jay had his face stuffed with his bar.

'So one day, I thought, that's my name. Say it loud. I'm Wiggie and I'm proud.'

'Good for you,' said Tulip, sincerely. Zac beamed at her.

When Wiggie dropped them off at the gates, Ali tugged Tulip's arm.

'Let's just walk back . . .' she started to say, but Jay interrupted her.

'You're bunking off,' he accused. 'Again.'

'Nooo, just dropped my . . . thing,' said Ali. 'Need to go back and get it.'

'What thing?' said Jay.

'None of your business,' Ali said, sharply.

'Her . . . girl stuff,' said Tulip. 'She's touchy about it.'

'Girl stuff?' said Jay.

'They've got a box of that stuff in the nurse's office,' said Zac.

'Could you be a bit less helpful?' snapped Ali. 'You're meant to be crippled by embarrassment!'

Unfortunately, by that time, the gym teacher had spotted them. He wasn't usually on the gate. He was so old-school he actually wore pressed shorts instead of trackie bottoms.

'Hey, you! Twins-one and twins-two! Stop dawdling and get yourselves into class!' He blew his whistle warningly.

Everyone was staring. There was no way the girls could quietly slip off.

'Break-time?' suggested Ali to Tulip, quietly.

'Break-time,' Tulip nodded. They did a tiny fist bump behind their backs.

'You look stressed, Mr Costas,' said Zac, as he walked past the teacher.

''Course I'm stressed, everyone's orf sick and the ones that are here are useless,' he complained. 'Malingerers, these new teachers. All they do is nap.'

It was a bit weird walking down the corridors. Everyone was quieter than usual. Instead of running around, lots of the kids were sitting on the floor. Some had their heads rested on their rolled up jackets, against the lockers.

'This is strange,' said Jay. 'There's something going around.'

'Well, it's not flu season,' said Ali flatly.

They'd got to class, and Mr Ofu was there. He was sitting at the desk. His head in his hands. His voice was trembling as he took the register.

They took their seats and answered cautiously.

'Sir,' said Tulip, politely. 'Perhaps you need to see the school nurse?'

'Ha!' said Mr Ofu, with indignation that turned into a yawn. 'I'd have to join the queue.' He finished the yawn, which turned into a sneeze, and then wheezed his way through the rest of the register.

'Sorry class,' he said. 'Must be my hayfever medication,' he yawned again. 'Doesn't usually knock me out like this.'

'Any other symptoms?' asked Tulip. 'Like a rash on your arm?'

'What?' said Mr Ofu. It was hot in the classroom, but he was wearing a long-sleeved shirt, which he'd pulled right down to cover his fingers.

He stood up to clean the board, and his shirt cuff fell back. Tulip breathed in sharply, and nudged Ali. There were bobbles on the back of one of his hands, trailing up his arm.

'Pustular rash?' they whispered, together. 'Jinx.'

'What did you say?' he said. Turning back.

'How far up does that rash go?' asked Ali. 'All the way to your BCG scar?'

'How did you know?' Mr Ofu trailed off. And stared at his gross hand.

'Well, maybe,' he said, 'I'll just pop down and see Mei Lin. I mean, Nurse Han.' He glanced at the clock. 'Why don't you all write me a piece in your project books about your plans for the Fayre tomorrow?'

He heaved himself out of the class. 'Tulip, you won the teamwork prize. You're in charge.'

'And I'll hand out the project books, Sir,' said Zac.

Jay shook his head in disgust. 'Volunteering again?' he muttered. 'It's like a disease with him. Think he just likes to be liked.'

'Ha! Not your problem,' said Ali.

As soon as Mr Ofu had left the room, Tulip went to the front, fiddling with her shoe by the chair where Mr Ofu's jacket was still hanging. She asked sweetly, 'Jay, do you mind being in charge for a bit? *Really* need the loo. Didn't get a chance to go what with all the chatting with *Wig-* . . .'

'Yeah, yeah, I'll do it,' said Jay, hurriedly, talking over her saying his dad's name.

'Thanks,' said Tulip. She left the room hurriedly.

'I'd better go with her,' said Ali. 'Chaperone.'

'She doesn't need a chaperone to pee,' said Jay. 'And besides, who's chaperoning you?'

'You're not very good at being in charge,' said Ali. 'No one's even started their piece,' and she pointed to the rest of the class. Most of them were drowsily nodding off into their textbooks.

When Jay turned to look, she just slipped out of the door.

'Hey,' said Zac, helpfully, calling out after her. 'The loos are the other way.'

When Ali caught up with Tulip, she asked urgently, 'so, what did you find?'

'What?' said Tulip.

'I saw you take something from Mr Ofu's pocket,' said Ali. 'When you were pretending to do your shoe.'

'Thought I was more subtle than that,' frowned Tulip. 'I just wanted to see if he'd been given any funny tablets. All I got was his phone.'

They had a look at it. There was a cover picture

of Mr Ofu with his partner on the beach. They were wearing matching rainbow T-shirts.

Ali shook her head. 'Matching T-shirts!' she said. 'What grown-ups wear matching T-shirts! Why not just print their faces on them. And add a flying pony!'

'Well, that's your Christmas present sorted,' said Tulip. 'But we have to be *riding* the flying pony. Definitely.'

Ali tapped the phone. 'Sturgeon!' she hissed. 'Stupid-Sneaky-Sturgeon!'

'What, is there a picture of him in a rainbow shirt, too?' asked Tulip, looking over.

'No, but a few missed calls,' said Ali. 'Why is he stalking our teachers? Look, there's a text message, too.'

Tulip read it out loud. 'Thank you for participating in my study. Let me know if you feel poorly again. Always happy to help.' She put the phone down. 'Ugh. The *monster*.'

'Big insincere slime-ball,' agreed Ali.

'Let's go to the nurse,' said Tulip. 'Mr Ofu said there was a line of sick people. Sounds like a clue.'

'So we're clue hunting?' said Ali. 'We're medics, not detectives.'

'We're both, now,' said Tulip. 'Medical detectives. Mum's sick and it's up to us to sort it.'

They got to the nurse's office. Mr Ofu was right about the line. The teachers were all sitting on chairs dragged into the corridor. Mrs Khan was talking earnestly to Mr Ofu, and she'd pulled up her sleeve to show him her arm. It was pus-covered and bobbly, all the way up to the round scar on her left arm. She saw them, and quickly yanked her sleeve down.

'What are you doing here, girls?' she said, sharply. The cross effect was a bit undone by her massive yawn.

'Feeling . . . vomity,' improvized Tulip.

'Oh yeah, so vomity,' said Ali. 'Got a funny tummy too.'

There was a yelp from the office, and Nurse Han bustled out, waving a thermometer. 'Did I hear vomity?' she frowned. 'And funny tummy?'

'So funny it could have its own show,' said Ali. 'Except no one would want to watch. It's pretty gross.'

Nurse Han pointed to a picture on the wall. It was titled the Bristol Stool Chart, with every kind of poo from a thick sausage, to rabbit droppings, to mush.

'Which one, girls?' she asked briskly.

'Definitely that one,' said Ali, pointing to the most disgusting looking.

'Vomiting and Diarrhoea!' shrieked Nurse Han. 'It's bad enough everyone's poorly today. But we can't have you infecting the school with norovirus. You have to go home, girls! NOW!'

CHECK PAGE 270 OF THE APPENDIX FOR THE MINI-MEDIX BLOG POST
TWINTERMISSION! TOILET TALK
OR WHAT DOES YOUR POO SAY ABOUT YOU!

'No problem,' said Ali. 'Is that OK, Mr Ofu?' He nodded weakly.

'Take care, Mrs Khan,' said Tulip, leaning casually on Mr Ofu's chair. She gently dropped his phone behind him. 'Hope you feel better soon.'

'You too, you two,' said Mrs Khan, more kindly.

They were quietly slipping out of school, when Jay popped up behind them.

'Where are you two going?' he said. 'Why aren't you back in class?'

'Why aren't you?' said Tulip, acting aghast.

'I left you in charge. Thought you were more responsible than that, Jay.' She tutted and looked convincingly let down. 'I'm not cross, Jay. Just disappointed.'

'What?' sputtered Jay. 'But you were the ones who . . .'

'So not cool,' said Ali, shaking her head. 'You'd better get back before someone ...'

'Starts another cola-storm,' said Tulip. 'You wanna be that kid? The one who let the Second Cola War happen?'

'Stop changing the subject,' said Jay. 'You're gonna be in so much trouble for leaving . . .'

'We've got permission,' said Ali. 'We've got vomiting and diarrhoea. We're infectious.'

'Twinfectious,' added Tulip, fist-bumping Ali.

'You are not!' scoffed Jay.

'Am so,' said Ali. 'Wanna share a straw? I'll prove it to you.'

'I'm not gonna let you leave the school,' sputtered Jay. 'It's . . . irresponsible.'

'Who's going to stop us?' asked Tulip.

And just then Zac turned up, racing around the corridor. Wheezing a bit, like he wasn't too fit.

Ali burst out laughing. 'Check out the back-up!'

'What's going on?' said Zac, looking from his brother to the twins. He pulled out a blue inhaler, and sucked on it. Tulip looked reproachfully at Ali for laughing at him. 'Thought you guys were trapped in the toilets, or something,' he said, when he'd caught his breath.

Jay wasn't looking at his brother. He was staring down at the twins. 'I'll call your MUM,' he said.

Tulip shrugged her shoulders. 'Good. Tell her we're on our way to the hospital to see her.'

'Now I KNOW you're lying. You wouldn't go to a hospital site with Vomiting and Diarrhoea,' said Jay. 'You'd infect people. Hah! That's it. I'll call your . . . your . . . Nan!'

This had a much more impressive effect than he and Zac anticipated. Ali and Tulip froze.

'Darn it,' whispered Tulip to Ali. 'He's good.'

Ali shook her head. 'Oh no. We're the good guys here,' she whispered back.

She tossed her ponytail, and walked squarely up to Jay, and pushed him against the wall with her fingertips.

'Look, you little *bug*,' she hissed. 'Our mum's sick. Our teachers are sick. And we have to find out why.'

'Your mum's sick?' asked Zac, looking at his brother. 'Seriously?'

'Deadly serious,' said Ali. 'You think I'd joke about something like that?'

'Sorry, guys,' said Tulip, pulling Ali back off Jay. 'But we have to go. For our mum. You can't stop us.'

'No, we can't,' said Zac, putting his hand warningly on Jay. 'But we can go with you.'

'What?' said Jay, Ali, and Tulip, together. 'Jinx,' they all said. 'Jinx, padlock, 1-2-3.'

'Did you guys practise that?' asked Zac. 'Let's go.'

They didn't speak as they followed him. They were all too shocked. Zac had never broken a rule or got a red card in his entire school career. He'd only got a yellow card when the whole of the class got one for being rowdy on a museum trip.

'Well, come on, then,' said Zac, signing the register responsibly. 'We're walking the twins home,' he called into the office, like it had all been arranged. 'We'll be back before break.'

'Thank you,' yawned the receptionist.

It was that easy.

CHAPTER 10:
SPYING ON MUM

They were on the train into town before Zac broke the jinx. 'So, Jay, Ali, and Tulip,' he said. 'Where we going?'

Ali sputtered in outrage. 'YOU aren't going anywhere, Tweedle-dumber!' she shrieked. 'You're going straight back to school, young man. Spit-spot!'

Tulip started laughing.

'What!' said Ali, turning on her furiously.

'You sound just like Nan-Nan,' she said. She turned to Zac, 'I've worked out your superpower, BTW.'

'You know, BTW actually takes longer to say than By-The-Way,' pointed out Jay. 'Like

WWW for World-Wide-Web.'

'OMG, you are soooo BOOOOORING,' said Ali, 'You really are Bore-Boy! Do people hire you for weddings to get the old people to nap?'

'Oh pull in your kitty claws, Ali-cat,' said Jay in a bored voice.

'So, what's my superpower?' asked Zac with interest, turning to Tulip.

'You can lie and get away with it,' said Tulip. 'I reckon you do it all the time.'

'No, I don't lie,' said Zac, simply.

'You see,' said Tulip, 'You're doing it right now. You're completely credible.'

'Don't care about his credibility,' said Ali. 'Point is, no one asked them along for the ride.'

'I didn't want to come,' pointed out Jay. 'I wanted to report you.'

'Their mum's sick,' said Zac, looking crossly at Jay. He gave him a hard, un-Zac-ish stare. 'Their MUM. We have to help.'

'You can't,' said Ali, flatly.

'Maybe they can,' said Tulip, unexpectedly. 'We can do more with four.'

'Five,' said Jay. 'Don't forget the cat.'

'Which cat?' said Ali, confused.

'Witch-*the*-cat,' corrected Zac, patiently.

'You know, that cat you've been pretending is your Nan's for some reason,' said Jay.

'How do you know she's not?' said Tulip.

'Because she's followed us from your road and you guys didn't notice,' said Jay. 'Look.'

He nodded towards the corner of the train carriage. Witch was there. Licking her paws. Looking pleased with herself. Like a poster that said: 'Me-Wow.'

'Also,' said Zac, 'she's a stray. No collar.'

'You see,' said Tulip. 'They're more observant than us.'

'Great,' complained Ali. 'Now we're stuck with Dumb and Dumber. They're probably only in it for the snacks.'

'Snacks!' Tulip grinned, and unzipped her bag. 'We can pay you in Pringles.'

'Wow,' Zac said. 'Check out all these additives! We never get to eat this stuff.'

'Wow,' Jay echoed, mockingly. 'You're easily bought.' He watched Witch slither along the other passengers' legs, including his own, before she leapt on Tulip's lap, and settled there.

Ali nodded in agreement with Jay. Which just felt too weird. 'OK,' she said. 'We've got a few stops before we change. So this is what's going on . . .'

Jay and Zac didn't interrupt. Or crunch the Pringles too loudly. But when they got off to change, they hovered on the platform indecisively.

'Whatsup?' asked Tulip, impatiently. 'You in or out?'

'In,' said Zac promptly.

'Go slow, little bro,' said Jay. He pushed his glasses firmly onto his nose. 'So let me recap . . .'

'I hate it when people recap,' said Ali.

Jay ignored her. 'You reckon that your mum's new boyf is some crazy-poison-peddler who's infecting your mum, the teachers, and maybe the kids at school with something that makes them sleepy and spotty. For some reason.'

'Um, yeah,' said Tulip.

'And now you want to go to the hospital to check on your mum, and basically spy on her at work.'

'Yup,' said Ali. 'She's gotta be Patient Zero. The first one infected.'

'Right. So I'm in, too,' said Jay. 'What?' he said, looking at the surprised faces. 'You're gonna do it anyway. And let's face it. You guys are about as sharp as a pile of puppies. You need me.'

'Yeah,' scoffed Ali, as she flounced ahead of them. 'You're the real shark in the tank.'

'Great way to say thank you,' said Jay, following her.

They switched platforms for the train that went towards the hospital.

'That's all phooey,' said Zac to his brother. 'You just like hanging out with them.'

'No I do not,' said Jay firmly. 'They're our NEMESI, remember.'

'You see,' Tulip nudged Ali, '*that's* the plural of nemesis.'

They'd been ignored on the train, but people started noticing them as soon as they got to the hospital. A couple of the porters recognized Tulip and Ali, and waved at them. A sweet lady with a clipboard asked them if they were lost. And an old bloke in a lab coat asked them where their parents were.

'On the ward,' said Ali. 'We're just getting snacks,' and Tulip and Zac waved their Pringles packets at him.

'We need a better cover story,' said Tulip,

under her breath. 'They won't let us wander around without an adult.'

Ali was looking at Jay, appraisingly. Taller than his twin by five finger-widths. 'You know what,' she said, 'you're almost as big as Mum. Admittedly, she's a bit of a midget, but . . . you were right. We *do* need you . . .'

'What are you saying?' asked Jay.

'Come on, *big* bro,' grinned Zac. 'You know exactly what she's saying.'

They followed Ali to the changing room near the operating theatres, and hid behind the vending machines, while she slipped in after someone who was chatting on their phone. Ali grabbed scrubs and masks and a fistful of hairnets, and walked out casually, with it all stuffed under her blazer.

'This ... is ... ridiculous,' said Jay, as he tugged the scrubs over his clothes. He hid his hair in the net, and put on the mask. It was one with a visor, so it covered his eyes, too.

'At least you won't catch anything,' said Zac cheerfully.

Ali handed out blue plastic aprons that she had pulled off a roll. 'Good idea,' she said. 'Pretend these are for infection control. And also these,' and she snapped on a regular mask and hairnet.

'Perfect,' said Tulip, looking at her reflection in her phone. Only her eyes could be seen. 'People won't recognize us.'

'And if anyone asks,' said Ali, inspecting Jay critically. 'You're our grown-up. Say you're taking us to our parents.'

'Fine, fine,' said Jay. 'I always knew that being bigger was going to bite me on the butt one day. Where now?'

'Neurosurgery on the second floor,' said Ali. 'You walk ahead.'

With Jay striding ahead in scrubs, no one stopped or questioned them. They made it through the glass walkway, and up the stairs. To the operating theatres. Double-doors swung open, and they saw a patient being wheeled out, and their mum, in her long surgeon's gown. They watched her yanking it off, and pulling off her face-mask, and bundling it into a bin of blood-streaked linen.

She came out. But there was a familiar silhouette, with a hat and shades, waiting for her.

'Sturgeon,' hissed Tulip. 'What's he doing?' It was so frustrating; Mum and Sturgeon had passed into the anaesthetic room on the far side of the operating theatre, out of earshot.

'Let's find out,' said Ali.

They snuck around the corridor. Mum and Sturgeon seemed to be arguing, which Tulip thought was encouraging. Mum hadn't had the energy to argue for a while. But then Sturgeon spoke to her, in a low voice, and patted her on the shoulder, and she stopped talking altogether.

Then something mad happened. Mum, their tired Mum, suddenly turned and dashed out of the room like someone running to a crash call. Her cloth bag bouncing on her shoulder. Ali and Tulip struggled to keep up with her.

'Where's she going?' panted Jay at their heels. Zac was following hard behind.

'What!' said Tulip, spinning around. She hadn't realized they were still with them. 'What are you guys doing here?'

There was a moment of confusion—the boys looked at her as though she'd gone mad.

'What, you mean, like on this planet, in an existential way?' asked Jay.

Zac flicked him on the head. 'We're helping you?' he hazarded instead.

'If we're following Mum,' said Ali, 'you should be tailing Sturgeon.'

'Oh,' said Jay. Annoyed, as that made perfect sense. 'Come on, slow-bro,' he snapped at Zac, and they dashed back the way they came.

Ali and Tulip followed Mum into the bowels of the hospital. She didn't speak or even nod to the many people who nodded and smiled at her. She just kept going with a relentless, robotic pace. Practically speedwalking.

'Has Mum been working out, or something?' huffed Tulip, in confusion. 'She's gone back from zero to hero.'

Eventually, Mum got to a lab, behind a closed grille, along a deserted corridor. The girls followed cautiously, as there was no one to hide behind. They saw some lab coats hanging outside the dissection room, and grabbed them. 'We can't walk together,' hissed Ali. 'Stay here. I'll go ahead.'

She strolled behind Mum, who was waiting at the grille, stabbing the button impatiently. Carried on until she got to the lockers at the end of the corridor. So that Tulip was one side, and she was on the other.

'Wait a moment, love, it's not a matter of life

and death,' called a voice, laughing at his own joke. The grille came up, revealing a square window opening, secured with wide bars, and a middle-aged man in a lab coat.

'Alright Minnie,' he said. 'How're your little ones? What brings you to our toxic little basement. They normally don't let us see the surface-dwellers.'

He was inspecting a sample, and his clipboard. He wasn't looking at Mum at all. He didn't notice Mum reach through the bars, and there was a flash of something in her hand. A tiny needle.

The man reached for his neck. 'Ooh, think I've been bitten?' he said, surprised. He keeled over the desk. Mum reached out for the ID badge hanging from his lab coat, and pulled it away from him on the long elastic cord.

She didn't look up or down the corridor. She didn't look at the security camera. She just tapped the ID on a pad, before letting it fly back to the man's coat. The steel door beside the grille beeped and let her through.

Ali and Tulip were left staring at the space that she had left. At each other across the white corridor.

'OMG,' they both whispered.

CHAPTER 11:
PATIENT ZERO

Ali tentatively approached the window, and saw the man slumped over his clipboard. The sample had rolled out of his hand.

Tulip picked it up. 'Pus collection: infected abdomen,' she read out loud. 'Ugh,' she said, dropping the tube.

Ali picked up the man's head by his thick hair. He snored. Loudly. And snot dripped from his nose.

'Ugh!' she said, dropping his head.

'He's just asleep,' said Tulip. 'Not out cold.'

'I saw a needle,' Ali said. 'Mum stabbed him with something. She's gone mental.'

'No,' said Tulip. 'This is Mum. Just 'cause she's been sleepy doesn't mean she's gone nuts.'

'Literally just saw her do it,' said Ali.

'Look,' said Tulip wildly. 'Maybe, Mum came marching down here 'cause she needed ... I don't know, that pus sample. Maybe she saw the guy get bitten by something, and she put out her hand ... to stop the bug. And maybe she took his ID to see how he is. She can't treat him through a barred window.'

'Well, where is she?' said Ali. 'She's not exactly rushing back to him.'

'She's gone to get ... a plaster. Or adrenaline. Or something,' said Tulip.

Ali nodded. 'OK,' she said. 'Let's go with that.' She stared at the door that Mum had gone through. 'Let's follow her.' She pulled at the man's ID card on the elastic cord, and tapped it to the pad. She released it too fast, so it wound back and whacked the poor man in the jaw.

'Sorry, Sir,' said Ali, blithely.

Tulip looked at her crossly, 'Come on,' she said.

They went through the beeping door, and saw a security camera filming a room at the back. Mum was there, in two views on the screens, gathering tubes from the fridges.

'Told you,' said Tulip with relief. 'She's getting stuff to treat his bite.'

But then something strange happened. Mum opened her shoulder bag, and filled her cloth bag with the tubes.

'She's not getting stuff,' said Ali. 'Is she ... nicking stuff?'

'Maybe,' said Tulip, reluctantly. She was watching Mum open a cupboard, which said 'Protected, Keep Out,' with a skull and crossbones. She took more vials, and added them to the stash in her bag. The man's snoring was getting louder.

'Maybe that's the chocolate cupboard?' said Tulip.

'Yeah, and I'm a flying pony,' said Ali. 'Duck!'

'Pony-Duck-what?' said Tulip. But Ali dragged her down. Someone else was approaching the room along the corridor. They could hear the tapping of smart shoes, a woman chatting on her phone. She didn't see the snoring man at the window, as she went straight to the door. She heard him, though.

'Working hard or hardly working, right, Arthur?' she called to the man, tapping her card on the panel, which beeped and let her through.

She strolled into the room where Mum was, and the twins stared at the screens, crouched on the floor.

The woman didn't even make it round the first set of fridges, as Mum's hand moved decisively and stabbed her in the neck. She slumped to the ground, and started snoring.

There was no mistake.

'I had no idea Mum had reflexes like that,' said Ali. A bit in awe.

And just then, Mum turned round. Swiftly. Like she'd heard them.

'Oh no,' said Tulip. 'This. Isn't. Good.'

'Let's go,' said Ali, tugging at the door. But she couldn't get it open. They stared at each other. The card for the entry panel was back with snoring Pus-Sample-Arthur.

'We need the card to get out!' Ali hissed. 'Don't let her see us!'

'She's gonna ground us,' yelped Tulip, commando-crawling towards the room where Arthur was dozing at his window.

'That's all that's bothering you?' said Ali, 'I'm more worried I'll end up stabbed like the Sleeping Beauties here.'

'Mum wouldn't attack us,' insisted Tulip.

'She wouldn't . . . she couldn't.' Doubt shivered in her voice.

Ali crawled on the floor after Tulip. But Mum had already opened the door to the supply room, back towards the exit.

'She won't see us,' whispered Tulip, hiding under the window. 'She's not gonna check on Arthur. She'll head straight out the door.'

'You're lucky you're funny,' said Ali, scornfully. 'She *can't* head straight out. She needs Pus-Sample's card to leave!'

But just when they thought that they couldn't escape, and it couldn't get worse, they heard a familiar voice. An unlikeable voice that sent a chill up their spines. 'Minnie?'

'Sturgeon!' they hissed.

Sturgeon must have opened the door to the corridor, as they heard it beep, and Mum raced out. 'See you at home, Sweetpea,' he said.

'Think I'm gonna be sick,' said Ali.

'Because Mum just knocked out two lab rats and stole a load of poisonous samples?' said Tulip.

'No, he called her *Sweetpea*,' said Ali, gagging. 'Yuck!'

They waited for Sturgeon to leave, but he

waited there. And then he said, 'You can come out, girls. She's gone.'

CHAPTER 12:
PROFESSOR STURGEON

Ali and Tulip remained stubbornly silent. But Sturgeon stayed right there.

'Look, you better get out of there, now,' he said. 'Or your mum'll get in trouble.'

'We're not here,' whispered Ali crossly to Tulip, who had shifted indecisively. 'He's got no proof we're here. He's bluffing.'

Just then, Tulip's phone rang. Out loud. It was Sturgeon calling.

'He's got proof now,' hissed Tulip. She'd never taken the battery out of her phone.

Ali shrugged, and answered it. 'Hi,' she whispered. 'We're at school. Bye!'

Sturgeon leaned towards the barred window,

and saw them crouched on the floor beside Arthur's chair. 'Ahoy,' he said to them, like an oldie worldie cartoon. 'You both come out here, and I'm going in there.'

He swiftly went to the back room, finding the woman Mum had needled in the neck, still slumped on the floor. He sat her up in a chair, and put her resting in the pillow of her arms on a table. Like she'd just nodded off while working.

Then he came back, to where Arthur was beginning to stir. He deleted the last few minutes of security footage from the screens, before coming back to the front of the window. The girls hovered behind him.

'Arthur,' he said, reading the ID badge. 'You napping on the job?'

'What?' said Arthur. 'No. Well, maybe. Something stung me, I think. Wasn't someone here?'

'Just got here myself,' said Sturgeon.

'And who are these little mites?' asked Arthur.

'Just kids,' said Sturgeon, off-handedly. 'Watching them for their mum.'

'Blimey,' said Arthur, 'Aren't those Minnie's girls? Mini Minnies! Haven't you grown?'

They nodded. 'It would be weirder if we hadn't,' pointed out Ali.

'Can't argue with that logic,' said Sturgeon. 'Come on, girls,' and he walked them round the corner.

'Sooo,' he said. A long-drawn-out note.

'Soooooooooo,' said Ali warily, mimicking him. An even longer note.

'*So*,' said Tulip shortly, cutting off Ali. 'You stopped Mum getting caught by that guy.'

'Yes,' said Sturgeon.

'And you stopped us getting caught by Mum,' said Tulip.

'Yes,' said Sturgeon.

'Mind telling us . . . why?' she asked.

Ali was looking at her furiously. 'Stop with the chit-chat! He's the enemy,' she hissed.

'Oh, I'm not the enemy,' said Sturgeon. 'And the reason is . . . obvious really. When I took on your mum, I took on you both, too. It's my job to look after you. Especially, when your mum is, well, not quite herself.'

'She's sick!' said Ali. 'And *you* did it! I know you did.'

Sturgeon suddenly looked sad. Like Nan-Nan when she had handed over the ice cream sundaes.

'Oh, girls,' he said. 'Yes, your mum IS sick. I don't know why she's doing this. Stealing supplies? Maybe it's a nervous breakdown. Or stress. But I promise you, I'll protect her. And we'll get her better. We'll get her back.'

And then he did the strangest thing ever. He crouched down, and gave them both a hug. It was squirmingly bizarre. They stood there stiffly, arms straight by their sides.

'Come on, girls,' he said. 'Let's get you both home.'

'It's not home if Mum's not there,' said Ali, shaking him off. 'It's just a leaky house with loads of stinking mushrooms in the fridge.'

'Yeah, what's with the mushrooms?' said Tulip. 'Never seen you eat them.'

Sturgeon looked shifty. But he always looked shifty, with his shades and his hat.

'I'll get you a hot chocolate first,' he said. 'You must be starving. You barely touched your porridge.'

Ali stopped, shocked. 'You actually saw how much porridge I chucked out?'

''Course I did,' said Sturgeon. 'It's my job. And Tulip, good girl for finishing all yours.'

Tulip beamed, as she always did when she

got a compliment, and then remembered who she was beaming at, and stopped abruptly. Like she'd been tricked.

Ali felt bad for her. It was all too weird.

'Guess hot chocolate couldn't hurt,' said Ali grudgingly.

'Good girl,' said Sturgeon, with his smile that showed too much of his teeth.

'And cake, too,' said Ali. Taking back control.

'You're definitely your mother's girls,' he said. 'She had doughnuts for dinner, last night.'

They went to one of the cafés on the ground floor. Sturgeon was ordering their hot chocolates, cupcakes, and a coffee for himself, when Tulip saw something shifting behind the plant pot in the corner of the café. In fact it was someone. It was Zac, waving surreptitiously.

'Look,' she hissed, nudging Ali.

'We're getting napkins,' Ali said loudly, and they went to the pot plant. 'What are you doing here?' she asked Zac. 'Thought we told you to . . .'

'You told us to tail Sturgeon,' said Jay, still disguised in scrubs and mask. He was sitting next to the pot plant. They'd missed him completely. 'That's what we've been doing. Really well.'

'Wow,' said Tulip. 'You're good.'

'I'm good at being invisible,' said Zac. 'Sometimes people don't notice me at all.'

'Wow,' repeated Tulip, less certainly. This seemed a little sad. 'So. Did you find out anything? Any weird stuff going on?'

'Not really,' said Jay. 'Unless you think it's weird that no one says hello to him?'

'Maybe they don't like him,' said Ali.

'It's more like they don't know him,' said Zac. 'Did he ever work here?'

'Dunno,' said Tulip.

'And it's not like we *talk* to him,' said Ali.

'You talked loads to him in the corridor, just now,' said Zac. 'We were behind the lockers.'

'That,' said Tulip, 'was literally the longest conversation we've had with him, ever.'

The girl behind the counter was asking Sturgeon for his name to put on his coffee cup. Sturgeon boomed out, 'Professor Brian Sturgeon, rhymes with Brain Surgeon . . .'

The girl shook back her beaded plaits. She said, quite patiently, 'Um, that's a bit long for the cup. So shall I just put initials? Is it P.B.S . . .'

Ali and Tulip cracked up. 'P.B.S,' Ali repeated. 'Poo-Bogey-Sick!'

'Putrid-Butt-Stink,' suggested Tulip. 'A bit classier.'

'Oh, grow up,' said Jay.

Meanwhile, Sturgeon had been lecturing the beaded-haired barista on why his name didn't abbreviate, forcing her to write it all in tiny letters around the cup. 'Furthermore,' he said, 'Brian Sturgeon is a fine example of nominative determinism. That means . . .'

'I know what nominative determinism means,' said the girl, less patiently. 'Your name defines your destiny. I'm doing a Masters in Literature.'

'Oh,' said Sturgeon, taken aback. 'Well, good for you.'

'Thanks,' said the girl, making his coffee efficiently. 'I'm touched by your validation.'

'Did he say he was Brian Sturgeon?' asked another man in the coffee shop, sitting in the comfy chairs next to where they were huddled. A cheerful-looking man, wearing a cream suit.

'Loud and long enough for the next ward to hear it,' confirmed Ali.

'Brownie Sturgeon!' the man called out, delightedly. He jumped out of his chair. Sturgeon jumped out of his skin. 'You've been Plaiced! How the fishy-in-a-dishy are you?'

Sturgeon recovered swiftly. And then looked at the older man dismissively. 'I'm sorry, have we . . . ?'

'Good one,' laughed the man. 'Acting like you don't remember the places.'

'No,' said Sturgeon. 'I don't, actually. Sorry. I'm not good with names, faces, or places. Were you at one of my many, well-attended conference speeches?'

'Names, faces, places?' repeated the man in confusion. 'Whatever are you bubbling on about, Brownie! I said *The Plaices*! I'm Pierce Plaice. You were at college with my big brother, Peter. You were the Fearsome Fishies! The Double-Bubble-Troubles! Stole punts together for midnight marauding . . .'

'Not ringing a bell,' said Sturgeon. 'Lots of people in college called Plaice, probably. Lots of punt-pinching.'

'Still a joker, I see, Brownie,' grinned the man. 'You mightn't remember me. I was just a squirt at school back then. But I know you know Peter! You were his best man!'

'Oh,' said Sturgeon. 'I was?' He pulled his hat further down his face. 'I mean, I do the Best Man thing a lot. I've got LOTS of friends.'

'You dated Betsy, our sister, for three years,' persisted Plaice.

'I did?' said Sturgeon.

'Our parents are in the same golf club in the village . . .'

'Oh. Right,' said Sturgeon.

'We used to dog-sit your puppies!'

'Of course!' said Sturgeon, acting like he was finally giving up the pretence. 'Ha-ha! Just having you on. Pleasure to see you, Plaice, after all these years, but I must be going. Got the kids, you see,' and he nodded towards Ali and Tulip. Gave them his weird cheesy happy-families photo face. Too many teeth.

'Oh, chillax, we're not in a hurry,' called out Ali, leaning back beside the plant pot. Zac gave a muffled yelp, where she squashed him in his hiding place, and she hastily straightened.

'Sturgeon's never told us about his friends,' added Tulip.

'Didn't know he had any,' commented Ali, looking at her nails.

'Life's treating you well, Brownie,' said Plaice. 'You're looking ten years younger than you should.'

Sturgeon said nothing. He gave a thin smile.

'And how are Pinky and Binky?' persisted Plaice. 'Adorable chaps. So friendly.'

Sturgeon looked blank. 'Were those . . . my . . . puppies?' he hazarded.

'Puppies? Good God, no. Your *parents*,' corrected Plaice. His smile was faltering. He looked quizzically at Sturgeon, at the shades and the hat, 'So how are they?'

'Dead,' said Sturgeon, shortly. He turned away, suddenly studying the café menu so hard it was like he had a test on it.

'Sorry to hear that,' said Plaice, taken aback. 'Hadn't heard a word on the village-vine. Was it recent?'

'Very,' said Sturgeon.

Plaice paused. His round face now looked concerned. 'I'm sure the wound must be rather raw, Brownie.' He leaned closer, and Sturgeon actually backed away, 'You know, Brownie, you've changed a lot from college. I really wouldn't have recognized you . . .'

'I had a bike accident,' interrupted Sturgeon. 'Needed surgery. Four plates plus ten nails in my face. Lost some skin, so got a bit of a facelift at the same time. So you wouldn't recognize me.' He shrugged, 'And *that* explains the youthful demeanour. It's not a secret. It's surgery.'

'Ah,' said Plaice. 'Knock on the head, too? Memory affected? Peter said you'd stopped practising. Gone off the grid . . .'

'So, where's Peter?' asked Sturgeon. Stiffly. 'I looked up the staff in this hospital. Didn't think ANY of my old friends or colleagues were here.'

'Oh, he's just back from two years in Australia,' said Pierce Plaice. 'I'm meeting him for coffee here. You can stay and catch up.'

'No! Isn't that what we've just done?' said Sturgeon, shortly. Plaice looked taken aback, and Sturgeon hastily added, 'Still, do give my regards to Peter. And to Betty.'

'Betsy,' said Plaice. 'I know that was a joke. Even with a knock on the noggin. You've got her name tattooed on your right clavicle.'

'Quite,' said Sturgeon, reaching for his collar. 'No one else knows about that, do they?' he asked a bit nervously. 'It's not in any of my interviews.' He patted the collar, as though reassuring himself it was buttoned shut, right up to the top.

'Betsy'll be delighted that Brownie's back in circulation. Rumour has it you'd become a bit of a recluse. Not quite yourself.'

'They've got that right,' said Jay, in a low voice. 'He's *not* himself.'

'So. Gotta go,' said Sturgeon, checking his reflection in the black mirror of his phone. Satisfied that his collar was high and his hat was low, as usual. He hadn't properly looked at Plaice in the face, and hadn't even taken off his shades, which were wrapped around his head.

Grabbing his coffee, he stalked out of the café, leaving the girls there. The only indication that they were meant to follow him was an irritated twitch of his head when he passed them. Ali and Tulip shrugged, and went to collect their hot chocolates and cupcakes.

'Did I upset him?' asked Plaice, as they walked by him. He seemed bewildered.

'Nah,' said Ali. 'He's like that with everyone. You actually got him on a good day.'

'But he seemed so . . . so . . .'

'Weird?' said Tulip. 'Mean? I guess we're just used to it now, so we don't even notice any more.'

'You're close to Brownie, are you?' asked Plaice.

'Not if we can help it,' said Ali.

'Hard to avoid him, though,' explained Tulip. 'He's moved in with our mum.'

'Why do you call him Brownie?' asked Zac, coming out from behind the plant.

'What?' said Plaice again. 'Another child! This place is teeming with them. Is this a school trip?' He looked around, like he was expecting more kids to crawl out from under the tables.

'Something like that,' agreed Jay, pulling off his hat and mask.

'Well,' said Tulip. 'Sorry about Sturgeon. And it was nice to meet you, Mr Plaice.'

'And you, young ladies,' said Plaice, gallantly bowing to the girls. He nodded to Zac, 'And to answer your question, young man, Brownie was Sturgeon's golf club handle. Brian Brownie Sturgeon.'

'Because of his brown ... hair?' suggested Tulip.

'He's not got brown hair,' laughed Plaice. 'He's more ginger than a biscuit! Just like his parents. No, because of his brown eyes. He was the only one in his family who had them.'

'Well, that was weird,' said Tulip, as they left the café. They could see Sturgeon on his phone, talking rapidly. He was double-geeking on his tablet at the same time, tapping away.

'What a noob,' said Ali. 'Creaky old dude. Doesn't even remember his best mate from uni. Or his parents' names.' She paused, thoughtfully. 'Nan-Nan did say that he was way older than he looked.'

'I didn't know he had puppies,' said Tulip. 'Does that mean *we* can get puppies?'

'I'm not sure puppies would get on with your Nan's cat,' said Zac. He was peering into Ali's schoolbag. Picking it up like it was too heavy. 'You know, the one you abandoned on the transport system.' Tulip suddenly looked a bit shifty.

'We don't actually have a cat,' said Ali. 'Remember.'

'You do now,' said Zac. He opened her bag to show Witch sleeping contentedly on top of her gym stuff.

'I *might* have dropped her in there,' admitted Tulip. 'I didn't want her to get lost. And my bag was full.'

'Gross! I'm burning all my kit when I get home,' said Ali. 'I'm burning the bag, too.'

'Focus on the fun stuff. Sturgeon's got a tattoo!'

Tulip sniggered, petting the cat, who purred softly, like a furry motor. 'Kept that quiet.'

'And he's been dyeing his ginger hair brown,' said Ali. 'Hair-larious! Probably hides the stuff in the bathroom so Mum doesn't see.'

Zac and Jay were looking at each other.

'What?' said Tulip. 'What are those weird little looks about?'

'They weren't weird,' said Zac. 'I'd say that they were more *darting* little looks. That's what I was going for.'

'What?' demanded Ali.

'I don't want to say you two are being thick . . .' said Jay.

'But there's no good way to end that sentence,' said Zac, apologetically.

'Care to share what you mean?' said Ali, bristling.

'Your main takeout of that little meeting was that he's old and forgetful and dyes his hair . . .' said Jay. 'That's all you got?'

'Well, what was yours?' said Tulip, crossly. 'What did you get?'

'I got that your mum's boyfriend,' said Jay, 'whoever he is . . .' he paused dramatically, 'isn't Professor Brian Sturgeon.'

CHAPTER 13:
EYES ON YOU

'Well that's just dumb,' said Ali bluntly. 'I think I'd know who he is.'

'I reckon that the stuff you *don't* know is a long and fascinating list,' said Jay. 'The guy's a fake! How could you not see it?'

'How could you not *not* see it,' countered Ali.

'What does that even mean?' asked Zac, looking between them like they were playing tennis.

'It means Ali can't stand that someone else worked out something she didn't,' said Jay. 'That guy's a bad guy. It's so obvious you can see it from space. He even LOOKS like the bad guy. All that's missing is a stupid little Hitler moustache to go with the stupid hat.

'It IS a stupid hat,' agreed Tulip. 'You know, they've got my attention,' she said to Ali, with interest, just like Nan-Nan had done.

'I'd rather that Sturgeon was the bad guy than Mum,' said Ali. 'But he's not the one we saw knocking out people and nicking dangerous lab-litter.'

'What?' said Zac.

'Oh, catch up,' said Ali, unfairly, as they hadn't told them what had happened in the lab.

'Go on, guys,' said Tulip, after she HAD caught them up. 'We're listening. Prove your hypothesis.'

'What's to prove? It's obvious,' said Jay. 'Didn't you see how freaked and rude he was acting?'

'Ah,' said Ali. 'You're just new to Sturgeon. He's freaked and rude all the time, like we said.'

'And he was hiding his face from his friend,' said Zac. 'He's not THAT hideous.'

'He hides his face from EVERYONE,' said Tulip. 'He literally only takes his hat off at home.'

'Does he even have a tattoo on his collarbone?' asked Jay bluntly.

The girls looked at each other. 'Ee-YEW!' they said together. 'Jinx, padlock, 1-2-3!'

'Well, does he?' asked Zac.

'Yuk,' said Ali. 'You think we'd ever look at him without his shirt on?'

'Double-yuk,' said Tulip. 'And it's not like he's ever gone to the pool with us.'

'So that's a no. You don't know,' said Jay, flatly. He persisted, in a businesslike way. 'Are his eyes even brown?'

'Um?' said Tulip, looking at Ali.

'Um,' said Ali, looking at Tulip. 'Dunno, really. Probably.'

'What?' said Zac, a little impatiently. 'You've never looked at his eyes?'

'Ee-YEW,' repeated Tulip. 'Why would we?'

'Who knows what colour people's eyes are?' argued Ali. 'It's a bit creepy, isn't it, to be looking into people's eyes? It's like you want them for a trophy.'

'*Your* eyes are brown,' said Zac. 'I know that.'

'You see,' said Ali. 'Creepy.'

'Not creepy,' said Jay. 'Basic observation.'

'Basic,' scoffed Ali. 'I've got ADVANCED observation skills.'

'You get competitive way too fast,' commented Tulip. 'You gotta work on that.'

'I can prove it,' said Ali. 'Go on, ask me a question. Ask me *anything*.'

'Fine. What colour are MY eyes?' said Jay, shutting them and turning away.

'Arrgh!' complained Ali. 'I meant a non-creepy-stalker question! Not planning to make them into jewellery so I DON'T KNOW,' she growled and stalked off, with her back to them all.

'She takes losing well,' commented Zac.

Jay played applause from his phone. Which Tulip thought was a little unkind.

Sturgeon spotted them still loitering outside the café, and began waving at them impatiently, from further up the corridor. 'Come on,' he yelled, snapping his fingers at them.

'Since when did doing that,' said Ali, snapping her fingers in Tulip's face, 'ever make anyone ever in the history of everything, do any stuff faster?'

'Never,' said Tulip. 'But it does make you blink.'

Sturgeon barked into his phone as they approached, 'Now we'll have to go to the next stage. Just hurry UP!'

'Problems with your research project?' asked Tulip, politely enough. Sipping her hot chocolate delicately. 'And what colour are your eyes?'

'Since when were you interested in my project?' asked Sturgeon.

'We're not,' said Ali, chugging her hot chocolate, wiping away a milk moustache. 'We're just trying to be nice. Nan-Nan said.'

Sturgeon breathed deeply, and put his fake-Sturgeon-smile on his face.

'Change of plans,' said Sturgeon, through his teeth. 'I can't take you home, now. I've got some research test subjects to check on. I'll call a cab to collect you and take you back. Stay here, and I'll text you the details.'

And he strode off. Stabbing his phone as he walked.

'You see,' said Tulip to the boys. 'Weird and rude.'

'Think we should follow him . . .' started Jay.

But there was a cry for help, and a flurry of activity from the café. A man was on the floor, and a couple of doctors were already kneeling next to him. The girls ran back, and saw that it was Pierce Plaice, collapsed.

'Sir,' one of the doctors shook him gently, but he didn't respond. The other doc called out, 'Did anyone see what happened?'

'He said he thought he'd been stung,' said

the braided barista, 'then he just fell to the floor.'

'Why aren't you starting CPR!' shouted another woman, bossily.

'Because he's stable,' said the doctor, confused. 'I've assessed him. His airway, breathing, circulation, well, they're all fine. It's like he's just . . .'

There was a loud, contented snore, and Pierce Plaice rolled into a comfortable position, his head in his arms.

'. . . asleep,' finished the doctor.

'Maybe he's a narcoleptic,' suggested someone else.

'Maybe not,' said Tulip, nudging Ali. She nodded. At the end of the corridor, there was a small woman in scrubs, walking away fast. It could have been Mum. But with the mask and the hairnet, it could have been anyone.

'Can't we wake him up?' asked Ali.

'Tried. He's out for the count,' said the doctor. 'I'll find him a bed to sleep it off. Whatever it is.'

They looked around, and realized that Zac and Jay weren't there. Tulip checked her phone, and saw a WhatsApp message from them. 'Started tailing Sturgeon. But he's got into a cab.

He asked for the zoo. 😶🤢🐼🐘🙈 Meet us out front.' 👍👍

'The zoo?' said Tulip, showing Ali her screen. 'That's . . . unexpected.'

'What do we do now?' said Ali. 'We can't leave Mum rampaging around the hospital nicking hazardous biological whatsits from labs and knocking out innocent NHS employees.'

But then, Mum appeared out of the crowd around the café. Like they'd summoned her by talking about her.

'Girls!' said Mum, shocked. 'What are you doing here?' She looked perfectly normal. But just a bit tired.

'Surprise!' said the twins, together. 'It's bring-your-daughter-to-work day!'

It was pretty rare for them to come out with an automatic utterly instinctive synchronized shared lie. Possibly unprecedented. They tried not to look too impressed with themselves.

'No, it's not,' frowned Mum. 'Did you practise that?'

'Happy Mummy Day?' suggested Tulip, handing her the squashed cupcake from the café, with half the icing licked off. Mum accepted it, and started eating it.

'No, it's not,' she repeated. 'But thanks, munchkin. I missed lunch.' She licked the icing just like Tulip. 'Try again.'

'Sturgeon brought us,' said Ali. 'Blame him.'

'Really?' said Mum. 'Brian brought you? Well, where is he?'

'He went off. To do some random stuff that was more important than looking after us. Checking his test subjects or something,' said Tulip.

'Oh,' said Mum. 'And he took you out of school and *left* you here?'

'Yeah, not cool,' said Ali. 'Definitely not cool with school. We'll be in SO MUCH trouble because of him. And I had to BEG him for these hot chocolates too.'

'My poor babies,' said Mum. 'I'll call Nan-Nan.' She looked a bit worried. 'I think I'm in trouble, too. They've been bleeping me in theatre for ages. I was only meant to be gone for ten minutes, while we called for the next patient. I've a horrible feeling he's on the operating table with a neck crick, waiting for me.'

'What were you doing?' asked Tulip, innocently.

'I think I was going to the loo and for lunch,' said Mum, 'But I definitely didn't make it to lunch, 'cause I'm starving. I just woke up in the doctors' mess. And someone's nicked my shoulder bag. It only had my commute-fruit and emergency chocolate in it, but you know . . . chocolate.'

'How are your hands?' asked Tulip, looking at Mum's single gloved hand.

'Bit of an itchy rash on this one,' said Mum, wiggling her fingers. 'Must be the soap in the theatre. Having a bobbly hand's horrible. Makes scrubbing in a nightmare.'

CHECK PAGE 272 OF THE APPENDIX FOR THE MINI-MEDIX BLOG POST

TWINTERMISSION! SCRUBBING IN

OR HOW TO WASH YOUR HANDS PROPERLY BECAUSE IT TURNS OUT YOU'VE BEEN DOING IT WRONG YOUR WHOLE LIFE!

'We'll call Nan-Nan,' said Ali. 'Don't worry, Mum. You go back to work.'

'What?' said Tulip, doubtfully.

'Yes, you should go back to work,' said Ali, 'definitely.'

'You sure?' said Mum.

'Absolutely certain,' said Ali.

'Hard to argue with certainty,' murmured Mum. She stifled a huge yawn. 'Alright then.'

She wandered off down the corridor. 'Theatres are upstairs, Mum,' said Ali, helpfully.

Mum waved sheepishly, and redirected herself, turning 180 degrees towards the stairwell.

'What,' said Tulip, 'was that! We can't send Mum back up to operate on people. She's not herself.'

'She's better than usual,' commented Ali. 'Think that was the best conversation we've had with her in a fortnight.'

'Really?' said Zac, from behind her. Ali jumped. She hadn't even spotted him coming back into the hospital. 'Our mum's there for *every* breakfast and dinner. And she reads to us every night.'

'A whole chapter,' added Jay, walking over.

'Your mum's life makes me sad,' said Ali. 'IMHO it shouldn't be any person's burning ambition to make meals for two bratty kids each day . . .'

'Hey!' protested Jay.

'And we've been free-reading from Year 2,' said Ali. 'Don't need to be read babybooks by some sad-stay-at-home in search of a hobby.'

'Shut up,' said Zac, seriously stung. 'Just 'cause your mum's happy to ditch you with some sleazy boyfriend.'

'*Your* life makes me sad,' said Jay pointedly.

'You shut up,' yelled Ali, balling up her fists and squaring up to the two of them.

Tulip pushed between them. 'Let's talk about MUM, please, she's about to scrape stuff out of someone's head!'

'Chillax,' said Ali, taking a deep breath, and unwinding her fists. 'If she can't do it, her boss'll take over. Mum'll step down, if they ask her, she won't put up a fight.'

'No, she won't,' agreed Tulip. 'Do you think it's weird how Mum just did exactly what you said?'

'Yeah,' said Zac, 'we saw. You told her to go back to work, and she did. You told her to turn right around, and she did.'

'Makes you wonder what someone else could say to her?' said Jay. 'If they sounded as certain as you.'

'Now you're saying it, yeah that's weird,' said Ali. 'It's like she's . . . in a suggestible state.'

'And she really doesn't know what she did just now,' added Tulip. 'Didn't seem bothered that she'd lost all the lab stuff she stole. After all that effort with the teeny needles.'

'Hmm, a suggestible state,' mused Ali. 'Do you think she's doing stuff without knowing . . . like she's under someone's spell.'

'Spell? Like Magic?' asked Zac.

'No, not *magic*,' said Tulip. 'Magic doesn't cause a blue bruise in an injection site.' She held out her fingers, counting their clues. 'So there's Sturgeon sneaking around the school. And the hospital. There's people acting like sheeple, getting sleepy-sick. And a pustular rash on their hands . . . like a drug reaction.'

'It's not magic,' agreed Ali.

'No,' said Tulip, 'it's medicine.'

'Bad medicine,' said Ali.

'Which takes a BAD medic,' said Tulip, finishing her thought.

'STURGEON!' they said together.

Jay and Zac didn't look convinced. But the hospital receptionist was waving to them. 'Girls, your cab's here.' And they saw a smiling young man outside, holding up a sign with A+T.

'Typical, Sturgeon couldn't even spell our names out properly,' said Ali.

'Hello, my young queens,' said the man, in a rich accent. He was holding a coffee in a reusable cup, which said, 'I am a reusable cup.'

'I am your driver,' he said, putting down the sign. 'I have been approved for cab journeys with unaccompanied minors. Please call your guardian to confirm my identity, to reassure your adult regarding any villainy or nefarious nonsense that may be afoot.' He passed them a sheet of paper, with the journey details pre-printed. 'Paid in advance. Terms and conditions apply,' he added.

'Hi, Momo,' said Tulip. 'Thought you'd gone to uni?'

'I am in the first year of my training as a social worker.' He bowed. 'This is an extra, as I am a people-person. I also do Deliveroo on my bike in the evenings, if you enjoy takeaway meals.'

Momo was a cab driver from the firm that Mum used in the days Before-Brian-Sturgeon, who'd pick up the girls and take them over to Nan-Nan's. He had been one of the local refugee kids Mum had mentored; she'd sponsored him for uni. Tulip was a bit surprised that Sturgeon was well-drilled enough to know to ask for him.

'Did Sturgeon ask you to come and get us?' asked Ali, who was thinking the same thing.

'No, your incompetent carer made an incompetent call to the firm of Central Cars,' said Momo. 'The wise controller directed the request to me, and I have come, although I have not yet had my coffee break.' He looked a bit sadly at his coffee. 'Which sucks.'

'Aw, that does suck,' said Tulip, with sympathy.

'Well, suck it down, cab-jockey,' said Ali bossily. 'We've gotta go to the zoo.'

'We're going to the zoo?' said Zac.

'Fine! You guys can come too,' she said.

'You are poets, and you know it,' said Momo. 'But I'm afraid I cannot take you.'

'What!' complained Ali. 'Hey, Momo, we're pre-paid!' She waved the bit of paper that he'd given her. 'Our cash our rules! You take us where we wanna go.'

'I am pre-paid to take you to *your home*,' said Momo. 'And these young men are not on my list to chaperone. I do not wish to put the kidnapping of schoolchildren on my paperwork. It would appear most unseemly on my forthcoming residency application.'

'Well, I think *that's* a teensy bit self-centred,' huffed Ali. 'It's not all-about-you!' Tulip kicked her impatiently.

'I think it's completely fair,' she said. 'Look at

it from Momo's point of view.' Momo beamed, showing his even, white teeth.

'Thank you, my queen.'

'But we would be so *very grateful* if you could take us to the zoo,' said Tulip, 'because our incompetent carer forgot that Mum's still working, our Nan-Nan's not back yet, so we'll be home ALONE . . .'

'Which is most irresponsible of him,' said Momo. 'I do not like that man.'

'And we can't leave our friends alone, either. They were our chaperones . . .'

'Even more irresponsible,' said Momo. 'He was *in loco parentis!*'

'He's definitely loco-coco,' agreed Tulip, twirling her fingers around her ears. 'So would you PLEASE take us to the zoo, because that's where he went. We're HIS responsibility. I'll text him we're on our way.'

'That would be the responsible thing to do,' agreed Momo. 'And it would also irritate him mightily. Come, children.'

As they walked to his cab, Zac nudged Tulip. 'That,' he said, 'was seriously impressive. No to Yes. You made *him* turn 180 degrees in about thirty seconds.'

'Told you,' she whispered back. 'It's my superpower. I can get people to do what I want. I just ask nicely.'

'Politeness isn't a superpower,' scoffed Ali.

'Jealous, much,' said Jay. 'Just 'cause it's something you've never mastered.'

Momo marched ahead of them, sipping his coffee, singing tunelessly, 'We're going to the zoo-zoo-zoo.' He called back to them, 'Sing with me children! The chorus requires harmonies!'

'This is gonna be a looong ride,' complained Ali. 'And brown, BTW!'

'What?' said Jay, squashing into the middle, in the back. But this time he didn't complain.

'Your eyes are brown, too. More like mud, really.'

'Hah! You looked,' said Jay. 'Didn't think you'd ever listen to anything I said, ever.'

'Already regretting it,' said Ali.

'Aww,' said Tulip. 'You guys are having a moment! I'm getting rainbow pony T-shirts for you two, too.'

Jay looked blank. 'Rainbow ponies? What's she going on about?'

'She thinks she's being cute,' said Ali. 'You get used to it.'

CHAPTER 14:
ALPACAS ASSEMBLE

Momo parked up at the zoo, and walked them towards the entrance. Sturgeon was pacing there, and when he spotted them, raced over with steam coming out of his ears.

'Ah, he looks most mightily inconvenienced,' said Momo, with a touch too much satisfaction. 'Goodbye my queens and kings,' and he bowed to them, with an extravagant triple-rolling-down wave. 'Momo, Away!' He sprinted back to his cab.

'He talks funny,' Zac pointed out.

'He came from a war zone at fourteen,' said Ali. 'What's your excuse?'

'But I like funny,' protested Zac. 'Most mightily. Don't you?'

Sturgeon stormed up to them, in a spitting fury. 'What-On-Earth-Are-You-Doing-Here!'

'Mum said,' Tulip answered sweetly. Unfazed. She much preferred him like this than when he was trying to hug them and being concerned about their breakfast. 'She was still working. Said we couldn't go home alone.'

'And BTW she wasn't impressed you'd brought us to the hospital and then ditched us there,' said Ali.

'I?' blustered Sturgeon. 'I? Brought you?' He threw his hands in the air like he was doing a demented dance-off. 'I didn't bring you to the hospital.'

'Whatevs,' said Ali. 'She still wasn't impressed.'

'Hey,' said Zac and Jay.

Sturgeon looked a bit shocked, noticing the boys for the first time.

'And who,' he said with haughty disdain, 'are you?'

'Zac,' said Zac.

'Jay,' said Jay. 'Duh.'

'That,' he said with gritted teeth, 'is not what I meant.'

'I get that,' said Jay. 'I mean, who's anyone really?'

'Yeah,' agreed Zac. 'I mean, who are you? *Really*?'

Sturgeon turned his back on them. 'What are they doing here?' he hissed at the girls, gesturing wildly behind him.

'Mum said,' shrugged Tulip briefly. 'Y'know.'

'Gnah!' said Sturgeon. 'I don't know! I don't care!' He opened his wallet, and peeled out some notes. 'I'm paying your entry fee. I'm giving you each twenty quid. Go to the shop and buy rubbish. I don't want to see you for two hours. I will find you at the gift shop, and take you home, and I don't want you to *ever* mention this little trip again. Clear?'

'Crystal,' said Tulip sweetly, with a thumbs up.

'Ever to mention,' said Jay, like he couldn't resist. 'NOT *to ever mention*. You split the infinitive.'

Sturgeon ignored him, and stormed away. Dust flying up behind his feet.

'Grammar geek,' Tulip commented to Jay. 'It's kind of amazing you've survived to Year 6 without a wedgie.'

'Let's go to the shop,' said Ali bossily. 'Spend the cash then search for clues.'

'I'm gonna follow him,' insisted Zac. 'He won't see me.'

'He won't,' agreed Tulip. 'It really is a superpower. It's like you're cellophane.'

'Fine, you go ahead,' said Ali. 'We'll buy stuff so it looks like we were hanging out in the shop. Message us where he is.' Zac nodded with a thumbs up, scampering away in the direction Sturgeon had stomped.

'Sturgeon had your mum's bag,' said Jay.

'What?' said Ali. 'No, he didn't. We'd have noticed.' Mum's bag was pretty distinctive. It said 'Girls Can Do Anything' in bright blocks.

'Same cloth bag,' insisted Jay, 'he'd just turned it inside out. But there wasn't anything exciting in it. Just fruit and chocolate.'

'Really?' frowned Ali. 'But what about all the test tubes and tiny bottles that Mum nicked? Where were they?'

Tulip piped up excitedly, 'His pockets!' She was practically jumping. 'They were all bulked up! Like they were when Witch attacked him!'

'Right. Five minutes max to buy stuff,' said Ali, 'and then we're gonna follow Zac following him.'

In the shop, Tulip was slowing them down, as

she couldn't choose between the four types of adorable and almost-identical baby owls.

'Shall I get you, or you, or you, or you!' she twittered to them. 'Twoot-twoo!'

'It's to-wit to-woo,' snapped Jay, impatiently.

'Enough with the infinitives,' said Tulip, just as impatiently, nuzzling the owls for softness-testing.

'You're correcting her owl pronunciation, now?' sniggered Ali. 'Didn't know you were fluent.' She picked up an alpaca, barely looking at it, and took it to the counter.

'Make that two,' shrugged Jay, grabbing another one. He was watching with disbelief, as Tulip cuddled all the baby owls she hadn't chosen so they wouldn't feel left out. 'Why does she like them so much?'

'Aw, she's only little,' said Ali. 'She'll always be half an hour smaller than me.'

'It's you, Cutie-Twootie!' said Tulip, as she finally chose an owl. 'I'm gonna call her Twoo!' She hugged it all the way to the counter.

'Finally,' said Ali. 'Put it with mine.'

'I like your alpaca!' squeaked Tulip. 'Is that Ali the alpaca! Ooh, she's got a twin, too!' she added, when she saw Jay's.

'Oh,' said Ali, looking at her toy. 'That's an alpaca? Thought it was a sheep.'

'Basic-observation-skills,' scoffed Jay. 'Better get another one for Zac, use up his cash.'

'It's like you don't even care about them,' said Tulip, scandalized. 'This is gonna be his new bed buddy! Cuddly toys are important.'

'They're not. They're just things,' said Jay flatly, picking up a third alpaca from the display. 'I care about real stuff. Like people.'

'Hey!' said Ali, slapping him on the arm. 'We care about people, too.'

'Yeah. Noticed what a people-person you are,' said Jay. His phone beeped. 'Zac says to head to this enclosure.' He pointed to a spot on the map.

'Is it near the owls?' said Tulip, hopefully. 'Cute baby owls?'

'Sorry,' he said.

'Let's google videos of cute baby owls on the way,' said Ali. 'I know you love them.'

'I know you're being sarcastic,' said Tulip, 'But I do! I really do! Tulip and Twoo, away!' She flew off out of the shop.

They found Zac hidden in the bushes behind an enclosure with dozing South American animals.

'Sturgeon's in there,' he hissed.

'Why are all the animals asleep?' asked Jay.

'I guess lots of animals sleep during the day,' said Tulip doubtfully.

She stared. There was something familiar about the way the animals were lined up. Heads bowed. She thought about the teachers that morning, outside the nurse's office.

'Research subjects!' she cried out. 'That's what Sturgeon said! He's been using the animals to test his . . . whatever it is.'

'Maybe he's done the beta test on animals,' said Ali, 'and he's moved onto humans!'

'That's brilliant,' said Zac.

'That's stupid,' said Jay. 'That's literally the most stupid thing I've ever heard.'

'I can prove it,' said Tulip, promptly. She pointed into the enclosure. 'Just give me a boost, to get in,' she said. 'And I'll look at the animals for a vaccination mark. A bruise. And a rash.'

The others looked at each other, unsure.

'Isn't that a little dangerous?' said Ali.

'Nope. Firstly, they're too sleepy-sick to attack. Secondly, animals *love* me,' said Tulip. And to prove her point, Witch, who'd been stirring in Ali's bag, jumped out, and straight into her arms.

'Well, I'll go, too,' said Ali, reluctantly. 'You guys happy to be lookouts?'

'More than,' said Zac, looking relieved. 'Don't like action. I'm more the sidelines guy, who says things like, "watch out, he's coming."'

'Yeah, and I have . . . allergies,' said Jay, looking with concern at the animals. 'Pollen and animal dander and fur and fluff and . . . and I *really* don't think you should go in . . .'

'Boost me,' said Tulip, ignoring him, and Ali boosted her over the edge. And Tulip tugged Ali after her. No one asked Witch, but she leapt in after them, too. Like she owned the place.

'They're definitely too sleepy-sick to attack,' repeated Tulip. More doubtfully.

'If you're wrong,' said Ali, 'we'll be trampled to pizza. Extra thin and crispy.'

They'd crept right next to the animals. Mostly alpacas, and a few others that looked more donkey-ish.

'They're too fluffy,' whispered Tulip, a bit fretfully. 'Normally I like fluffy, but I can't see a bruise through all that.'

'Sturgeon must've injected where he couldn't get kicked?' suggested Ali. 'Try the back?'

Tulip nodded. She carefully patted an alpaca, and when he didn't stir, she slid onto his back. She pushed her fingers through the hair on the back of the neck.

'Found it!' she whispered excitedly. 'Bruising, and an icky pustular rash!'

'X marks the spot,' said Ali. She crawled over another alpaca. 'Yup, this one too!' She took a photo, and saw something glittering in the sun.

'Hey, what's this?' said Ali. She found a cracked glass tube in the alpaca's fuzz. She held it up, and squinted at it in the sunlight. 'Smells funny,' she said, screwing up her nose.

Witch had been licking herself at a safe distance from the alpacas and the donkey things. But she suddenly raised her head. On high alert. Pointed her black muzzle towards Ali.

And then she leapt.

'Witch, noooooooooo,' Tulip yelled. Witch was leaping at Ali's alpaca with claws flared just like she'd leapt at Sturgeon. She landed on the alpaca's rump, digging in hard. And the alpaca woke, and snorted with fury, kicking out at Tulip's alpaca ahead of her.

'Noooooooo,' repeated Ali, as both their alpacas reared up, and Witch began attacking her, while she swung the glass tube around wildly to avoid dropping it, gripping on to the alpaca by his fluff. 'Bad cat! Bad, bad cat!'

'What's going on over there?' yelled Jay.

'Want me to draw you a picture?' shrieked Ali, clinging on for her life. The other alpacas were getting kicked and waking grumpily.

'Chuck that thing away,' said Tulip, who was clinging on too.

'What thing!' yelled Ali.

'That thing in your hand,' yelled Tulip. 'THAT'S what he had in his pockets. That's what Witch wants!'

Ali chucked it away, as far as she could. And Witch leapt after the tube, racing for it while it flew in the air.

'What was in that?' she yelped.

But Witch wasn't the only one racing. Ali's alpaca, Tulip's alpaca, and the others started chasing down Witch.

'Watch out! He's coming back,' yelled Zac. 'Seriously! It's Sturgeon.'

'You know what,' yelled back Ali, 'I'm thinking our cover was blown, already.'

A pair of zookeepers had begun racing towards them, too. And Sturgeon, walking briskly through the enclosure, right in front of them, stopped in horror. Witch dropped the glass in her mouth, and leapt at him again, going for his packed pockets.

'He's got more,' said Tulip. 'That's what he's been using! He's been injecting them.'

'The animals are crazy for it,' yelled Ali.

Sturgeon started running away, chased by Witch, a blur of fur and claws. Witch was chased by the alpacas like some avenging army, with Ali and Tulip clinging on tight and screaming. And the zookeepers were chasing the alpacas, yelling and waving dart guns.

'This-is-not-cool,' shouted Ali, between bumps.

'Just-don't-let-go,' yelled Tulip.

'Don't-let-go,' sneered Ali, still being brutally bumped. 'Thanks-for-that. Genius.'

They watched Sturgeon flailing at the edge of the enclosure, before he finally fought off Witch, and legged it over the edge. Witch disappeared after him. But the alpacas showed no sign of slowing. 'They're going to mow down that fence,' shrieked Ali.

'Zac! Jay!' yelled Tulip to the boys, who had been running around the enclosure edge after them, 'Boys! The *toys*!'

'Not-the-time-for-cuddly-toys!' yelled Ali. 'You've got a problem!'

'The toys! Show them the toys!' insisted Tulip.

Jay dug out their two alpacas, and Zac waved them. 'Here, alpacas,' he called. 'Look! Cute baby versions of you!'

Madly, the alpacas slowed down. They turned as a herd, and went towards the fluffy toys. And the alpacas carrying Tulip and Ali arrived at the edge of the enclosure first, and began nuzzling the super-soft alpaca toys.

'Aw,' said Tulip. She slid off her alpaca, and climbed over the edge of the enclosure. 'See? Everyone likes cuddly baby toys. Even more than they like chasing narcotics.'

Ali slid off too, much less gracefully. 'That was *horrible*,' she complained.

'That,' said Zac, 'was the coolest thing ever!'

'Reckon Sturgeon's been stabbing the alpacas with that stuff,' said Tulip to the boys. 'Poor drugged-up things are addicted.'

'He's been getting it from the hospital . . .' said Ali. 'Mum's been nicking it for him.'

'How does he vaccinate the alpacas in the first place?' asked Jay. 'They're not exactly peaceful around that stuff. How'd he get near them?'

'Do alpacas like mushrooms?' asked Zac. 'Someone's left a whole box of them here, next to the veg for their feed.'

'No one likes mushrooms,' said Ali.

'We do,' said Zac. 'We even eat them raw, in salads.' And he picked up one, polished it against his blazer like an apple and tossed it in the air to catch it in his mouth.

Tulip reached out and caught it neatly instead in her hand. 'You don't want that.'

'What?' he said.

'They're bad mushrooms,' she said. 'From a bad medic.'

Ali nodded. She'd got there, too. 'The mushrooms from our fridge,' she said. 'Betting Sturgeon tampered with them. Put something in them that calms the alpacas down, before he needles them.'

The zookeepers had rounded up the other alpacas, and were coming towards them.

'What do we do now?' said Zac. Backing swiftly away.

'What we said we'd do,' said Ali, striding off and ignoring the shouts from the zookeepers. 'We'll meet Sturgeon at the gift shop.'

CHAPTER 15:
THE GINGER INTRUDER

Sturgeon was already there. Speaking to three people in suits. 'I can't thank you enough for helping the children,' he was saying. 'Rounding up those crazed creatures.'

The zookeepers arrived, and heard this last bit with a lot of indignation. 'They weren't crazed creatures!' said one woman, in her wellies and work overalls. 'They were peacefully sleeping, and these crazy kids INVADED the enclosure with their insane CAT!'

'It's not *our* cat,' said Ali, rebelliously. 'We're not the boss of it.'

'We're so sorry,' said Tulip. 'We were just looking for our grown-up. We were . . .' and she blinked, with what looked like real tears, 'a bit FWIGHTENED. Left all alone in the shop.' The lisping was a nice touch.

'We were,' agreed Jay, and his eyes were streaming too. His allergies were kicking in, but the grown-ups wouldn't know that. 'So, so FWIGHTENED.'

'You left them alone, Professor Sturgeon?' said one of the suited men, crossly. 'How could you!' The reproach was apparent, and Ali and Tulip nodded fiercely in agreement. 'When we agreed to your observation of our animals, we did not think it involved babysitting services . . .'

'It won't happen again,' said Sturgeon, with gritted teeth. 'I'm not letting them out of my sight for A MOMENT.'

He knelt down, and gave them one of his creepy happy-families hugs, in a public charade of affection. 'I'm so sorry you were scared. Why don't we go for ice cream?'

Ali tore away from him.

'You KNEW he was in the enclosure?' she yelled to the suits. 'He's a Brain Surgeon! What work d'you think he's doing with alpacas?'

'Observing, Sweetie-Pie,' said Sturgeon, with a forced smile. 'You wouldn't understand.'

'Try me!' said Ali.

'Who wants ice cream?' said Sturgeon. 'Yes! Let's go.'

Sturgeon bundled them all in the car, and drove in stony silence back to their bit of town. A muscle near his jaw was twitching. He got to the girls' house first.

'I suppose you two can walk from here?' he told Zac and Jay, rather than asking them.

'Sure,' said Zac, but Tulip nudged him. She messaged them rapidly, KEEP HIM BUSY FOR A BIT.

'Except I'm a bit scared after all that zoo stuff, and Jay's got allergies, and Dad can't come and get us and our mum's been so poorly . . .' Zac improvized rapidly.

'We're still FWIGHTENED . . .' agreed Jay, glancing at the message. 'And I really need my anti-allergy meds . . .' That bit was true. His eyes and nose were streaming. And he was getting a rash on his neck. 'It's my urticaria,' he said, pointing to the weals. 'I'm itching like mad.'

CHECK PAGE 276 OF THE APPENDIX FOR THE MINI-MEDIX BLOG POST

EMERGENCY TWINTERVENTION! ALL ABOUT ALLERGIES

OR WHAT YOU DO WHEN ALLERGIES ATTACK!

'Oh, fine,' snapped Sturgeon, without sympathy. 'You two, in the house!' he barked at the girls. 'I'll be back in five minutes. Don't do ANYTHING until I get back. Don't touch anything, don't talk to anyone, don't . . .'

'Chillax,' said Ali. 'We get it. *Don't* plus any verb. We'll finish the speech ourselves if you've got somewhere to be . . .'

'Argh!' grouched Sturgeon, and sped off with the boys.

They went up to the door, and Tulip dropped Witch on the front wall. 'Shoo, Witchy,' she said. 'Go home.'

'Don't think she's got one,' said Ali. She kicked their welcome mat glumly. 'Jay said my life makes him sad.'

'He didn't mean that,' said Tulip.

Ali sat on the step. 'I'm cross 'cause he's right.

Mum's dating some complete psycho, and we're home alone. Again.'

'It's not all about us,' commented Tulip. 'You should stop being down on them because their mum's suddenly stay-at-home and doing all the school stuff. They're right, you're not good at looking, or listening. Zac just said that their mum was sick, you heard that right?'

'No,' said Ali. 'Wrong way round. He's helping us because OUR mum's sick. Duh.'

'You're hopeless,' said Tulip, kindly.

She pressed the bell. She knew Mum wasn't home, but she thought that Nan-Nan might be listening. She was right.

'Girls,' said Nan-Nan distractedly, on the intercom. 'What are you doing back so soon?'

'Long story,' said Tulip, 'but it's a good one. With alpacas.'

'Sure it'll be fascinating,' said Nan-Nan. Her voice was echoing like she was moving around. 'I'm kind of in the middle of something . . .'

'Could you come over?' pleaded Tulip. 'We're home alone, and Sturgeon's gonna tell us off.'

Nan-Nan sighed. 'Sure, munchkins. I'll be round in a tick. Before you know it. But best stay downstairs. Grab yourselves something in the kitchen.'

'Why downstairs?' asked Tulip.

'And grab what?' said Ali, grumpily. 'Mum's not cooked in forever. I've literally had dessert for dinner and breakfast. I'd KILL for something savoury. Just cheese on toast. I'd even have salad. Anything that's not mushrooms . . .'

'Sturgeon's poisoned the mushrooms,' explained Tulip. 'They're the only thing in the fridge.'

'I can manage cheese on toast,' said Nan-Nan. 'See you in a bit.' She sounded out of breath, like she was walking fast. Except that Nan-Nan didn't walk.

'Are you . . . exercising, Nan-Nan?' asked Tulip.

'Absolutely. That's exactly what I'm doing,' said Nan-Nan promptly, hanging up on them.

Tulip opened the door, and hurried Ali in. 'Come on,' she said. 'We're wasting time. I wanna search the spare room. Before Sturgeon comes back.'

'We can't get in,' commented Ali. 'It's locked.'

Tulip strode up to the door, and tried it. 'Maybe it's motion-sensored, like Nan-Nan's door.'

'What?' said Ali irritably. 'No, it's not.'

'Catch up,' said Tulip, and she gave the door an experimental kick.

'Oh,' said Ali, getting it. She stood next to Tulip, ready to kick, too. 'And catch up is my line! Stop stealing my lines . . .'

'Sure it was someone else's first,' said Tulip. 'Come on, on three! One, two . . .'

She stopped. She could hear someone inside the room. Moving around. The creak of a window being opened. Ali's eyes were wide, she heard it too.

'THREE,' Ali yelled, and they kicked at the lock together. The door shuddered, but it stayed stubbornly shut. They could hear frantic movement, stuff falling to the floor and smashing, and then urgent steps . . .

'ONE-TWO-THREE!' yelled the girls together, and they kicked again, and this time, the lock broke, and the door flew open. They were just in time to see a skinny woman, all in black like a cat burglar, in a fedora hat and dark glasses, with a wild wig of red hair, leap onto the hastily cleared desk, and out of the window. They ran to the window, and saw her swinging expertly down the drainpipe, out over the neighbour's garden, and then she was gone.

'Well, that was stupid,' said Tulip, breathing heavily. 'The next time a stranger's in the house, instead of surprising them in the act, we should just walk out of the door.'

'She could've had a gun,' agreed Ali. 'I just wasn't thinking.'

'What was she looking for?' said Tulip. 'The room's trashed.' She poked the box from that morning with her feet. It was full of broken bits of glass. 'Test tubes?' she said.

'Maybe we *should* walk out the door,' said Ali, as they heard a car pulling up outside. 'Sturgeon's gonna kill us. He'll think this was us.'

'It shoulda been,' said Tulip. 'Only Ginger-Wig-Woman beat us to it.'

Sturgeon strode in, and straight up the stairs.

'What!' he said. He clutched his head in disbelief, as he looked around the room. 'What! What HAVE YOU DONE! I was gone for FIVE minutes, and you've, you've, you've . . .'

He staggered about the room. 'I need to sit down,' he muttered, but the chairs were toppled over. He leaned back against the broken door, and sank to the ground, his backside landing with a crunch on the box of broken glass. 'Why-why-why . . .' he was muttering.

Ali and Tulip looked at each other. And decided with a nod that the only thing to do was to tell the truth.

'Flattered, to know what you think of us,' said Ali. 'And flattered that you think we could do all this in five minutes. But this wasn't us.'

'It wasn't,' he repeated, in disbelief.

'We came upstairs, and there was someone here. A woman. She left through the window,' said Tulip.

'Impossible!' he said. 'Who could know . . .'

'Know what?' said Ali. 'You're up to something seriously dodgy, aren't you?'

'What!' said Sturgeon, 'I'm not going to dignify that with an answer.'

'Whatevs,' said Tulip. 'I'm gonna call the police. Breaking, entering, she probably nicked a load of whatever you got here, too.' She got her phone out, but Sturgeon jumped up and took it from her.

'No,' he said. 'Really no need. No need at all.'

'What?' said Tulip. 'But someone's just wrecked the room? Why wouldn't you report it?'

'An innocent man would report it,' said Ali, pointedly.

'I AM innocent,' protested Sturgeon. 'I'm the VICTIM here, and I don't want an army of flat-footed police officers going through my years of precious research! And it would upset your mother, too.'

'What?' said Tulip. 'Are you saying you don't want to tell Mum, either? That's crazy.'

'This, the zoo, the hospital,' said Sturgeon, 'has to be secret. Our little secret.'

'You sound seriously creepy when you say that,' shuddered Ali, backing away.

'. . . because you need to protect your mum,' said Sturgeon. 'And you need to protect me too. I'm with the good guys.'

'Hah!' said Tulip. 'We're the good guys, not you! You couldn't be more of a bad guy if you lived in an evil black tower with evil lightning around it and wore a black hazmat suit with your stupid black hat and if you were called Von Evil De Ville . . .'

'Stop saying EVIL,' said Sturgeon, covering his ears like the word was painful. 'You'll keep quiet for your mum's sake.'

'But not for you,' said Ali. 'Don't think you

can sleaze your way into our lives and replace our dad just because you're stupidly rich and . . .'

'I couldn't replace your dad,' said Sturgeon, solemnly. He stood up. Pulled off his hat. Showing his short brown hair. Pulled off his shades. Ali and Tulip gasped, but it turned out not to be a big moment.

His eyes were brown, after all.

'I AM your dad.'

CHAPTER 16:
WHO'S THE DADDY?

Tulip was open-mouthed with shock. Ali picked up Tulip's dropped jaw, and closed it, with an eye-roll.

And then Ali did a slow handclap, 'Really good, Sturgeon. Seriously, how stupid do you think we are? Our dad's in the cemetery behind Nan-Nan's place.'

'Why do you think your mum and I moved so fast?' said Sturgeon. 'She and her husband couldn't have children. Because of his tumour treatment. I was an anonymous donor. We found out when we met at that conference. I discovered I had two kids. And that she'd found a father for hers.'

'Why wouldn't she say?' said Tulip. The bit about Mum and Dad needing a donor didn't sound that unlikely. She knew their dad had been fried with chemo meds for the big C that had invaded his brain.

'She has her reasons,' said Sturgeon. 'I respect that. But maybe keeping this secret from you is the reason for her . . . erratic behaviour. Pilfering lab samples. Sleeping all day. The mind has complexities we cannot begin to fathom . . .'

It sounded like the start of one of his recorded lectures. He played them in his room sometimes. Repeated them out loud.

But then, Tulip surprised Ali. Horribly.

'OMG,' she said. 'It all makes sense. Gosh, Daddy!' and she flung herself at him, and gave him a huge hug, that took him by surprise, too.

'What are you . . .' started Ali.

'I think, deep down,' said Tulip, her face squished against his shoulder, 'on some level, I always knew.'

'You did?' said Sturgeon.

'You did?' said Ali. 'What level was that? Didn't think they dug the sewers that deep?'

'And Nan-Nan told us to be kind,' said Tulip. 'Maybe she knew too . . .'

'You know he's really ginger, right?' said Ali. 'Look at us? How could *our* genetic dad be ginger!'

'You leave him alone,' said Tulip, turning on Ali. 'Just 'cause he's a minority . . .'

'I'm really sure that ginger doesn't qualify as a minority,' argued Ali.

'Whatevs, he's suffered enough!' She patted Sturgeon kindly on the back. 'This'll be our little secret.' And she jerked her head towards Ali. 'I'll keep this one in line. Don't worry.'

'Thank you, Tulip,' said Sturgeon. He smirked at Ali. She glared at him, crossed her arms, and stomped away. 'You've always been my favourite.'

'Favourite deluded butt-kisser,' muttered Ali.

They heard the doorbell, and Nan-Nan opening the door with her keys. 'Girls!' she called. 'Nan-Nan's here.'

'Not a word!' whispered Sturgeon. He ran down the stairs, 'Thank goodness. Just in time! I just have to pop out and replace my . . . supplies. Give them dinner, will you?'

'Hello would be nice,' commented Nan-Nan.

Sturgeon looked briefly abashed, but then she said, 'Fine. Off you go. Spit-spot!'

Sturgeon obeyed immediately, as though afraid she would change her mind.

CHAPTER 17:
X MARKS THE SPOT

As soon as he left, Tulip dropped the wide-eyed act, and wiped her mouth where it had touched his shoulder. 'Yee-uck,' she said. 'No one should be that close to the Sturgeon.'

'You,' said Ali, half-relieved but mostly furious, 'are *unbelievable*!'

'You mean *believable*,' said Tulip. 'Sturgeon believed it, didn't he? And so did you.'

'A little bit,' admitted Ali, grudgingly.

'What's going on?' asked Nan-Nan, wheeling herself over the threshold. 'Wash your hands, and catch me up. I'll put on cheese toast and a nice salad.'

'I love you, Nan-Nan,' said Ali, sincerely. 'Cheese toast!'

Ten minutes later, Tulip and Ali ran into the kitchen.

'I'm so starving I'd eat a stuffed toy, if it came with ketchup,' Ali was saying, but then she stopped, and held her nose. 'Ee-yew!'

'Nan-Nan,' asked Tulip sweetly, 'what smells so gross?'

'Noooo!' yelped Ali, looking around wildly. 'She's been looking at more *recipes*!' She looked accusingly at Nan-Nan. 'You said cheese toast and salad!'

'That's what I made,' said Nan-Nan, briskly. 'A delectable salade du chèvre chaud. Melted goat's cheese, on a nice baguette, and the salad has sweetcorn and asparagus.'

'Asparagus!' said Tulip glumly. 'You're killing me.'

'You ruined cheese toast,' complained Ali. She slumped at the table and crossed her arms, 'I hate you, Nan-Nan.'

Nan-Nan dramatically clutched at her heart, and collapsed over the table, with her tongue lolling.

'You really dead?' asked Tulip.

Nan-Nan made a gurgling, rasping sound.

'Ok, hate might be a bit strong,' admitted Ali.

'And I guess asparagus isn't likely to actually kill me,' said Tulip.

'Of course it is,' said Nan-Nan, sitting up promptly, 'And of course it won't!' She scooped up a bit of gooey cheesy baguette. 'Hah, hit me where it hurts, why don't you? My *cooking* skills!'

'It's Tulip's split infinitives that hurt most,' said Ali. 'To actually kill? Really?'

'Correcting grammar?' said Tulip. 'Just like Jay? Explains why you've both got so many friends.'

'Hey, I've got plenty of . . .' but Ali trailed off. She hadn't got a single vote in the Class Teamwork Award. Tulip had pity-voted for Zac. 'Oh shut up,' she said. 'I hate you! Shut up.'

'Right,' said Tulip. She pushed her plate aside, and turned to Nan-Nan. 'Ali's a bit busy hating me, so I'll catch you up.'

Nan-Nan's eyes barely flickered when Tulip told her about the hospital, and Witch hitch-hiking the ride, and Mum on her mad lab-ransacking mission. She just tutted when they got to the bit about the cat burglar.

'You don't seem that surprised?' said Tulip.

'Oh, what?' said Nan-Nan. 'Absolutely, all of that is completely new news to me! All of it!'

'Give it up,' said Ali, who felt she'd been quieter longer than she'd ever been in her life. 'You don't act surprised any better than you act dead. And FYI, the next time you wanna fake a heart attack, talk about pain up your left arm. And start sweating.'

'I *might* have been following your progress,' said Nan-Nan. 'I have my little ways. Thought it best, after what you said about Brian.'

'Aw, you were protecting us!' said Tulip, reluctantly attempting her goat's cheese baguette. Her stomach was rumbling, and Nan-Nan was showing no signs of removing it and replacing it with something normal. The stinking goat's cheese oozed right off the bread and slid in a stringy mess into the salad. 'Oh yeuch, it's like flubber!'

'Like eating melted socks,' agreed Ali, rolling the cheese goo around her plate. She put a clothes peg on her nose. And then she took a bite. 'I can deal with that,' she shrugged, 'if I don't have to taste or smell it,' and she swallowed it down fast.

Nan-Nan beamed at her.

'Actually,' said Nan-Nan, eating her goo with

sincere relish, 'I was protecting HIM. I thought you'd poison him or something, thinking you were protecting your mother . . .'

'Hey!' said Ali. 'We're not the bad guys here! We're the good guys! We're not in the black hats!'

'Good, bad. Whatever. I've never paid much attention to that distinction,' said Nan-Nan airily. 'But manslaughter would've been a pain for me to cover up, even for terrible tots like you. Don't even want to think about the paperwork.'

'How were you following us?' said Ali. 'You've injected us with some sort of tracker, haven't you?'

'Oh, please,' said Nan-Nan. 'How could I?' She busied herself with mopping up the juices from her salad, humming happily.

Ali and Tulip looked at each other significantly. Nan-Nan had just avoided answering the question again.

'So,' said Ali. 'How *did* you have eyes on us?'

'So,' said Nan-Nan, talking over her at the same time. 'I take it you've had a little rummage about in Brian's room?'

'Of course not,' said Tulip, affronted. 'We told you that was some crazed ginger lady. She jumped out of the window.'

'Probably Sturgeon's secret ginger twin,' said Ali. 'The less evil one.'

'She wasn't Sturgeon's twin,' commented Tulip. 'The hair was like a clown wig. She was more like a circus artist, dangling down the drainpipe.'

'That's nothing,' said Nan-Nan. 'You should've seen *my* act, before I got wheels. I could feed a baby with one hand and hog-tie a bad guy with another . . .'

She looked straight at them. 'I don't think you quite heard me. I said you've had a little rummage in Brian's room?'

'But we just said . . .' complained Ali.

Nan-Nan silenced her with a raised eyebrow. 'And if not, why not?' she said pointedly. 'Go! Tear that place apart. Find all the stuff that's hidden from my cameras. Who could tell what Ginger did, or you?'

Ali and Tulip looked at each other. 'Let's do it,' said Ali. 'There might be evidence.'

Tulip nodded. 'If there's anything there, we'll find it.'

When they got to the top of the stairs, she realized that was way easier to say than to do. The room had been trashed. There were papers all over the place. Bits of glass. Broken vials.

'Really hoping he doesn't have dangerous chemical waste in here,' said Ali. She began picking through stuff.

'It's like our room used to be, during the Lego wars,' commented Tulip, 'when we used to use our floor for a trap.' She began going through a pile of papers, stacking them neatly as she looked through each piece.

'Hey!' said Ali. 'Stop that! You're tidying up.'

'No, I'm not,' said Tulip, adding another paper to the stack.

'You are,' said Ali. 'You'll give us away. The cat burglar definitely didn't leave stuff in nice little piles,' and she kicked over the stack that Tulip had made.

'This is ridiculous,' said Ali, about a minute later. 'We won't find anything here.'

'I'm sure we will,' said Tulip. 'It's only a little room.'

'There are only three brain cells knocking about in that *little* head of yours,' commented Ali, 'and you've not found ANY of those yet.'

'I get you're frustrated,' said Tulip, 'so I'm gonna ignore that. You're probably cranky because you're still hungry. Go eat your salad.'

'NO!' said Ali. 'That crazy cheese is plotting

world domination. It's probably already squelched off the plate.'

Tulip shrugged and carried on.

'Whadya looking through, there, anyway?' asked Ali, sifting the floor debris.

'Nothing much,' said Tulip, cross-legged on the floor. 'Sturgeon's bank statements. He's still sending money to some random place in the Pacific.'

'Boring!' said Ali.

'Well, what've you found?' said Tulip crossly. 'A map with X marks the spot?'

'Nah . . . just research papers,' said Ali. 'Experiments on lab rats and stuff. Probably keeping tabs on his old mates. You know, the rats.'

'He's got files on *himself* here,' said Tulip. 'Cuttings from every paper he's written, every interview. The only photo is that one when he was a student.'

'Check the clown-college hair,' commented Ali, looking at the shot. 'Ha-ha-Hair-larious!'

'Now you're making fun of him because of his hair?' Tulip shook her head, reproachfully. 'Maybe that's why he straightens it. 'Cause he got made fun of.'

'*You* make fun of him because of his hat,' pointed out Ali. 'Hair, hat. Basically no difference. It's the stuff keeping his big stupid head warm.'

'You know,' said Tulip, 'he really doesn't look like his teen pic.' She frowned again. So hard that a little lump puffed out between her eyebrows.

'His nose is definitely different. It's bigger than that,' she said with authority. 'How would a horrible bike accident and surgery GROW his nose?'

'Puh-leeze,' said Ali. 'You're sounding like Jay.' She mimicked Jay's voice, 'Sturgeon's not Sturgeon. I know that because my mum makes me gluten-free pancakes and carries me around the house on a throne with my face hand-stitched on the cushions . . .'

'Still,' said Tulip, 'those files on himself. And look, he's made notes. With post-its and stuff. Why would you need to REVISE your own life, like it's your specialist subject?'

'Maybe he's just an egotist. It's all about HIM,' said Ali. 'He listens to his own interviews, too.' She flicked through his files idly. Like she was beginning to agree with Tulip, but she didn't want to admit it.

'One thing I can't see here,' she added grudgingly, 'is any mention of a Betsy tattoo.'

'This interview says he was going off the grid, to focus on his research,' said Tulip. 'Probably this place in the Pacific where he's sending the money.'

'Off-the-Grid had enough of him, like the rest of us,' commented Ali. 'Check the date. He met Mum just after that article came out.'

Tulip went over to the desk, and on the floor, was a school photo. It had fallen out of one of the books.

'Already checked that,' said Ali dismissively. 'That's nothing. It's not even Sturgeon's school photo, it's Mum's.'

'Ooh, it is,' said Tulip. Mum was easy to spot as she was front row and her hair was still the same. Short dark fluff. Like she couldn't be bothered to brush it. 'Guess they made her sit in the front because she was the shortest.'

Ali experimentally pulled at one of the drawers. It was locked. She put her foot against the desk, and yanked it with all her weight. The drawer flew out, and she went toppling over.

'Was that worth it?' said Tulip, drily.

'Nope,' said Ali, looking at the contents of the

drawer. 'Just some chocolate, and fruit. Brown banana. Green apple.'

'Wait,' asked Tulip, frowning. 'Isn't that Mum's missing chocolate? And her commute-fruit?'

'Maybe Sturgeon had the munchies,' shrugged Ali. 'He nicked it from her at the hospital, remember.' But then she saw what was next to the fruit. A loaded syringe.

'Tulip,' said Ali. 'I don't think he's just tampering with the mushrooms.'

'Evidence!' said Tulip, triumphantly. 'I knew we'd find it!'

'We?' scoffed Ali. 'Think you mean, *Me*. Credit-grabber.'

'Ooh, you're SOOO grouchy when you're hungry,' said Tulip. 'I'm looking under the carpet, Mum never fixed the loose bit of floorboard.'

'I'm even considering eating the poisoned banana,' said Ali, picking it up and looking for syringe marks.

Tulip went to the corner of the room, and carefully lifted up the carpet. One of the floorboards had been wobbly for ages. Mum had marked it with a cross of masking tape to be fixed down, but they'd never got round to calling someone to sort it. Mum avoided DIY, as, for a surgeon, she was pretty clumsy with heavy tools. Once she'd whacked her finger with a hammer and couldn't operate for a week.

Tulip slid her library card down the side of the loose board with the taped X, flipping it up. There was a gap there where they used to hide stuff.

She gasped, as she hadn't expected to find anything at all. But there, in the shoebox-sized hole, was an actual shoebox. She opened it carefully. It was full of tiny vials.

'X marks the spot,' said Tulip, more in wonder than triumph. She pulled out a vial, inspecting it carefully. It was marked with a plain sticky label, with ADT typed on it.

Tulip showed it to Ali, frowning a mountain, 'What does ADT mean?'

Ali just did her *I-Dunno* shrug. 'More glass tubes full of random stuff,' she commented. 'That's refreshing. Any idea how to find out what these are?'

'Nope,' said Tulip, replacing the board. She closed the box neatly. 'But I know a Nan-Nan who can.' Ali had drifted back towards the photo of Mum, smiling up from the desk in her blue school shirt and trousers. Mum had basically worn the same outfit since she was thirteen.

Nan-Nan was yelling something up the stairs. 'Get down, girls, he's . . .'

'Yeah, yeah, quit nagging, we're done!' yelled Ali.

'Mission accomplished,' confirmed Tulip.

'You know, I don't like leaving this photo in the room,' Ali commented.

'Me neither,' said Tulip. 'I don't know why he nicked it. It's meant to be downstairs in Mum's school album.'

'You deaf, munchkins?' hollered Nan-Nan. 'I said, Get Down! He's coming up the road!'

'We're coming,' called Tulip, decisively grabbing the photo. Ali picked up the box full of the tinkling vials, and they ran out of the room to the top of the stairs.

'Damn, I'll have to stall him,' complained Nan-Nan, spotting them on the landing. 'Don't let him see you were up there!'

CHAPTER 18:
BLACK TEA RHYMES WITH CREEPY

Nan-Nan rolled out towards the front door, blocking Sturgeon coming back into the house, bumping right into his knees.

'Ooh, Brian, isn't it lovely weather!' she exclaimed heartily. 'Now be a dear and get me some of that lavender by the wall.'

'Weather?' said Sturgeon, bemusedly. 'Wall? Lavender?' He tried to squeeze into the house, but Nan-Nan twinkled up at him, pushing him back out.

'Yes, dear, lav-en-der,' said Nan-Nan, stressing all three syllables, like she was congratulating a kid for managing a difficult word. 'I need it for my cupcake recipe.'

'Lavender?' said Sturgeon. 'For a recipe?'

'You're repeating yourself, dear,' said Nan-Nan. 'Let's work on that.'

'I don't really have time . . .' started Sturgeon.

'Spit-spot,' said Nan-Nan. 'Oven's already on.'

Ali and Tulip crept down the stairs, and were in the kitchen by the time Sturgeon had turned back up the front path. Nan-Nan really had switched on the oven.

'We need to look like we're baking stuff,' Tulip hissed to Ali, pulling on Mum's apron.

'We don't know how,' complained Ali.

'Improvize!' suggested Tulip.

Sturgeon was coming down the hall, and Tulip yanked a bag of flour from the cupboard, and ripped it open clumsily, so that white clouds exploded into the air, and settled like snow onto their hair.

'Is that all we do?' said Ali. 'I'm down with that,' and she tugged the box of eggs open, and began smashing them into a cereal bowl. 'Ee-yew!' she said holding up her eggy-goopy hands, so it dripped to the floor. 'It's like snot when it's not an omelette.'

Sturgeon walked into the kitchen, and saw

them, covered in egg-goop, bits of shell, and flour.

'What are you doing . . .' he started.

'Baking,' said Ali. 'Duh.'

'You're *baking*,' he complained, skidding on spilt egg white on the floor. 'Shouldn't you wait for your mother?'

'Puh-leeze,' said Tulip, brightly. 'You know that Mum doesn't bake.'

Shaking his head moodily, he dumped the lavender on the counter, and mooched upstairs.

'Don't bother me,' he snarled over his shoulder. 'I've got a lifetime of work to salvage from my wrecked office . . .'

'Oh, poor Brian,' said Nan-Nan, rolling back in. 'Would you like me to fix you something? A cuppa?' She spotted Ali's eggs in the bowl, and pressed her lips together, like she was trying not to laugh. 'Maybe a nice mushroom omelette? Looks like we're halfway there.'

'No!' said Sturgeon. 'Not the mushrooms! They're . . . special.'

'Quite right,' said Nan-Nan. 'So many poisonous varieties. Even the ones in the fridge aren't above suspicion.'

'What?' said Sturgeon, twisting around swiftly.

'What *what*, dear? You're repeating yourself again,' said Nan-Nan. 'Must be the stress. Just the tea, then. A nice milky brew.'

'No milk!' barked Sturgeon, stomping up the stairs.

Sturgeon closed the spare room door behind him with a bang, and Nan-Nan looked up with satisfaction, before rolling into the kitchen.

'Impressive, girls. You were right about those mushrooms,' said Nan-Nan. She clapped her hands together gleefully. 'And now I have an excuse to make lavender cakes. Saw a *lovely* recipe trending online.'

'Nooo,' groaned Tulip. 'Not more recipes! You've already ruined cheese toast.'

'Don't ruin cake!' warned Ali, 'Don't!'

'Oh, pish posh,' said Nan-Nan. 'I think you'll find the cakes most impressive, too.'

'Before we bake,' said Tulip, 'we found some stuff upstairs.'

They showed her the glass vials, the little bottles marked ADT.

On closer inspection, they were also marked with a strange symbol. A dot. That was crossed out.

Nan-Nan tapped the label with her finger,

thoughtfully, before propping up her phone with the lavender recipe. There was a smiley man in a ridiculously white shirt making the cake, without a single bit of egg-goop or flour on him.

'Any idea what that might mean?' asked Nan-Nan, picking bits of eggshell out of the bowl. 'A crossed-out dot?' She glanced at the phone, with the ingredients list swishing under Smiley-Man, and scooped sugar and margarine and flour on top of the eggs.

'An allergy symbol?' suggested Tulip. 'These bottles are for medication. They've got lids that you can stick a needle in. Draw up for an injection.'

'Hmm,' said Nan-Nan. 'And you've already told me your hypothesis about what he's injecting.'

'Something that makes people sleepy,' said Ali. 'It gives them a gross pustular rash too, down from the injection site. Like bubble-wrap. Pop goes the measle.'

Nan-Nan nodded thoughtfully, and then passed them the bowl and a couple of wooden spoons. 'Give that a good beating, girls.'

'Gross,' said Tulip, inspecting the curdled mess. 'Looks like a cupcake vomited.'

'Beat harder, then,' said Nan-Nan, demonstrating, with both spoons. Her biceps bulged, and the scrambled eggy-greasy-goop began to look like creamy cake mix.

'Narly, Nan-Nan,' said Tulip, sincerely. She took a spoon and copied.

'Sturgeon's been tampering with Mum's food, too,' said Ali, licking her spoon instead of helping. 'He's nicked her emergency chocolate and commute-fruit from her bag.'

'He's been doing what!' said Nan-Nan, sharply. 'Tampering with my daughter's chocolate! Oh, it is on! I promise he will RUE the day . . .' She gathered up the bottles. 'I'm gonna get the girls in the lab to check these out!'

'That's so cool,' said Tulip. 'You've got girls in the lab!'

'Contacts from the old days,' shrugged Nan-Nan. 'Everyone in the SWAT team had them.'

'Did you have a computer guy in a room, who told you where to go?' asked Ali. 'Like when you were on a mission. Running down the street chasing someone . . .'

Nan-Nan looked appalled. 'You've met me, right? When did anyone, ever, tell ME where to go. I do the telling.'

As if to prove her point, she nodded at the school picture Tulip had left on the side. 'Pop that back in the album, dear. It wasn't your mum's best hair day, but I still don't think she wants it egged-up.'

She leaned back, and took in their floured appearance properly, and burst out laughing. 'You're too young to go grey, dears.'

'Haha,' said Ali, shaking the flour off her hair, and into the cake bowl.

'That's gross!' said Tulip, watching her. 'No way am I gonna eat that. Why don't you just get your Ali-cat to spit up a fur-ball into it too?'

'Oh, you two were never going to eat it, anyway,' said Nan-Nan. She pulled out cupcake cases, and briskly split the mixture in two bowls. And poured one of the vials into one set, and left the other.

'What are you doing, Nan-Nan?' said Ali, interested. 'So one set has ADT, and the other doesn't?'

'Well,' said Nan-Nan, sprinkling the lavender over the cake mix in both bowls, 'Sturgeon has his little experiments, and I have mine.'

She did a final whisk, and then efficiently plopped the mix into the two sets of cupcake cases and put the cupcakes in the oven.

'Don't let me leave one of the tainted cupcakes in the house,' said Nan-Nan. 'You know your mother will hoover them up. I don't think the woman even chews.'

'Once, for her birthday, we made her a cupcake smoothie,' nodded Tulip. 'She was soooo happy.'

Nan-Nan laughed, and picked up the kettle. 'I did promise I'd make Brian a cuppa,' she said significantly, 'and I always deliver on my promises.'

'*I'm* not taking it up,' said Ali and Tulip together.

'Jinx, padlock, 1-2-3,' they said together, crossly.

'No, *You* take it up,' they said, still together.

Nan-Nan looked at them with interest. 'Creepy twins who speak in unison,' she commented. 'Not a cliché at all.' She poured the tea onto a bag.

'He said NO MILK, didn't he?' said Nan-Nan.

'Yeah, Sturgeon doesn't have milk,' said Tulip.

He didn't have biscuits with his tea either. He *never* had cake. He didn't even like having cake in the house. So Mum now ate them out of the bag on the way home.

Sometimes Tulip wondered what he and Mum could even talk about. They had nothing in common. Mum was all about cake and cuddles and he wasn't about either.

Brain-doctoring stories didn't seem enough to get them through a first date, let alone into the same terraced house.

'And we're not creepy . . .' said Tulip. She remembered the photo album, and opened it to replace Mum's school photo.

' . . . 'Cause we know Creepy,' said Ali, 'We live with him like 24/7. *Black* tea. That's creepy. Creepy-tea. Practically rhymes.'

'Finishing each other's sentences, now?' said Nan-Nan. 'That's on the creepy spectrum right there.'

Tulip was staring at the album, biting her lip in confusion. She flicked backward and forward through the pages. 'Well, that's weird,' she said.

'Something not-weird today would be the weird thing,' said Ali. 'What level of weird could Mum's mouldy old school mugshots be bringing to the party?'

'I can't find the gap to put the shot in,' said Tulip. '*All* her school photos are here.'

'There must be one,' said Ali bossily. 'Give it to me, Noob.'

'You're the noob,' said Tulip, grabbing the album back. 'There isn't a space. And look!' she pointed triumphantly at another shot in the album, 'There's the same photo! Check her mutant-fluff-haircut!'

'Hey!' said Nan-Nan, sharply. 'She chose that cut!'

'Aww. To punish you?' enquired Ali sweetly.

'Point is,' said Tulip. 'This isn't *Mum's* school photo at all. Her one's stuck in here. And she's written the class and year on it.'

'So it's *someone else's* school photo,' suggested Ali. 'Someone else in the shot. Maybe Sturgeon stole it off that ginger cat burglar, and she wanted it back.'

'I doubt that anyone would shinny up a drainpipe and scuff her best spy-sneakers just to steal a spotty-swot-shot,' said Nan-Nan. 'Let me have a look at that.'

'And how did you know she wore spy-sneakers?' asked Ali.

'The Nan-Nan-cam,' said Nan-Nan, promptly. 'I'm recording upstairs, remember?'

She looked at the photo. And frowned a

zigzag mountain, just like the girls. 'No,' she said. She frowned again, and squinted. 'Maybe?' And then she said, 'NO, that's just *ridiculous*.'

'Spotted one of Mum's old mates?' asked Tulip.

'Not exactly,' said Nan-Nan, scanning the shot on her phone. 'I'm going to put this through a bit of facial recognition software . . . it's probably nothing. But I better check it out.'

'Tell us!' said Ali. 'Or we'll nag.'

'When Minnie was a teen,' said Nan-Nan, 'there was this socially awkward kid who kept coming round. Showing her his science stuff. Dedicated his big win to her at the Science Fair . . .'

'So far, so boring,' yawned Ali.

'Then it turned out he'd nicked the whole project from somewhere else,' said Nan-Nan. 'He got really upset when he was found out. Swore revenge on the school. Said he'd show them all. A bit derivative, I thought.'

'What did he do for revenge?' asked Tulip. 'Prank the pool with a plastic poo?'

'Nothing at all,' said Nan-Nan. 'He moved away, I think. Didn't see him around after that.'

'Which one was the weird kid?' asked Tulip with interest.

'Easy to spot,' said Nan-Nan. 'He's the chubby one hiding behind his hair.'

'Ooh, got him!' said Tulip.

'I've got him too,' said Ali, excitedly. 'Check the curtains in front of his face.'

'Ooh,' said Tulip, like she was disappointed in Ali. 'That's a bit unkind. Maybe he was shy. Or had acne.'

'They ALL have acne,' pointed out Ali, 'they're teens. All teens are spotty-sweaty-swotty.'

'Poor Evelyn,' Nan-Nan commented. 'He didn't really have friends. I think Minnie just felt sorry for him.'

Ali and Tulip caught each other's eyes, and began sniggering.

'What?' said Nan-Nan, sharply.

'Evelyn!' cracked up Ali, howling with laughter. 'A guy called Evelyn.'

'Was his surname Von Evil De Ville?' asked Tulip with interest. 'I've always thought that would be a great villain name. Evilyn Von Evil De Ville.'

'It was Sprotland,' said Nan-Nan, checking her phone, as the facial recognition app beeped. She added airily, 'unfortunate kid. Not sure why I'm mentioning him.'

'Wait a min,' said Tulip, looking shrewdly at

Nan-Nan. 'Do you think he has something to do with this?'

At that moment, they heard Mum's key in the door.

'Hello darling,' called Nan-Nan. She turned back to the girls. 'I really wouldn't know, dears. *You* brought him up.'

Ali and Tulip had lots to say to this, but were prevented by Mum bowling into the kitchen. 'Oh Mama-bear,' she shrieked happily, bending to give Nan-Nan a hug. 'You made cakes!'

'Don't get too excited,' said Nan-Nan. 'They're ALL for the Fayre tomorrow.'

'Oh,' said Mum. But then she cheered up. 'I'm meant to go to the Fayre tomorrow,' she said. 'I can buy all the cakes I want! Finally!'

'Brian still doesn't like cakes in the house?' asked Nan-Nan, disapprovingly. She pulled the cupcakes out of the oven. 'Frankly I think that's a teensy bit controlling.'

'Says he's watching his weight,' complained Mum. 'He doesn't want the temptation around. Once I left a bag of doughnuts out, and they ALL disappeared overnight, and he went running the whole next morning to work them off. Blamed me. I literally have to finish my cake-carbs on the *doorstep*. Which reminds me . . .'

She went to the fridge, and poured some milk into a plastic bowl, and put it outside.

'There's this homeless cat who keeps hanging around on the step. Feel bad for the poor thing.'

'She LURVES Sturgeon,' said Ali. 'We should put food out for her too.'

'Really?' said Mum. 'Oh, that's so sweet. It's nice he's making furry friends. Normally animals loathe him.' She kissed the girls and hugged them both, lifting them right up. And when she'd put them both down, she spotted the black tea. 'And you made tea for him too? You really are the nicest girls in the world!'

She took the tea, and swanned upstairs with it, 'Tea, Brian!' she called.

'Nicest girls? Was she being ironic?' asked Ali, with genuine confusion.

'Not everyone's you,' said Tulip. 'You gotta learn to take a compliment.'

She spotted Nan-Nan rolling out the door, with the freshly baked cupcakes already baggied up. 'Hey, Nan-Nan? Where are you going?'

'Well, ask a silly question,' said Nan-Nan infuriatingly, and she rolled out of the door.

CHAPTER 19 :
EVIL-IN-SPROTLAND

Tulip dutifully dumped the baking stuff in the dishwasher, while Ali stared at her phone.

'Hey, Screen-eyes,' complained Tulip, 'why am I always the one clearing up after us?'

'Nan-Nan's your mentor,' said Ali, not looking up. 'She said cleaning up messes was good training.'

'Well, why don't *you* train,' said Tulip, grabbing Ali's phone. She saw a vast WhatsApp stream from Zac and Jay. And a few failed video calls. She clicked to call them back.

'I'm *already* trained up,' said Ali. 'When something's perfect you can only make it worse.'

Jay and Zac had appeared in the screen. Tulip

could only see their heads and most of their nostrils.

'Whoa,' she said. 'Too much information! I can seriously see all the way to your brains.'

Jay pulled back hastily. 'Did Ali just say she was perfect? Seriously, she's like one big motivational cat poster. Saying I'm PURR-fect.'

Ali's face froze.

There was a deadly silence.

They all waited for the Ali-explosion.

And then she exploded. With laughter. 'OMG,' she shrieked. 'Jay did a funny! Jay's making JOKES now. And it wasn't awful.'

Tulip grinned with relief. And a little pride. 'You see,' she said, giving Ali a hug. 'That's called growth.'

'Yeah, I guess people can change,' said Ali.

'It would be weirder if they didn't,' said Zac. 'I always thought Jay was funny. But mean-funny. Like you.'

'We were just being mean-funny about this total science-nerd,' said Ali.

Jay made a frustrated cough. 'I'm right here, you know. I'm literally sat right here in my bedroom.'

'Oh chillax, Noob,' said Ali. 'We weren't talking about YOU.'

'It's not your bedroom,' protested Zac. 'It's OUR bedroom.'

'We're on my side,' said Jay. 'Or would be if you didn't keep shifting the masking tape.'

'Mum says it's not nice to build walls,' argued Zac.

'It's tape! You can literally step over it,' said Jay, gesturing to the floor. Jumping over the tape and back again. 'Your space, my space, see!'

'Ooh, so that's your room,' said Ali, nosing her face into the screen. 'Nice dump you've got there!'

'Nice dump you've got there, too,' said Jay, peering a bit closer. 'Like your yellow walls.'

'Really,' said Ali, doubtfully, looking around. The walls in the kitchen were peeling because of damp seeping in from the weedy garden. There was a hole in the corner of the ceiling, where the bath had leaked because Tulip and Ali were playing Flood-versus-Waterfall, and Mum had stabbed the swelling bubble of water on the ceiling with a screwdriver and caught the water in a washing-up bowl. That was about as handy as Mum got.

Sturgeon had said he'd sort it.

But Sturgeon said a lot of things.

Most of them stupid.

'Well, your curtains are nice, too,' said Tulip. She wasn't lying. They were.

'Oh, thanks,' beamed Zac. 'Mum made them. She let us pick the fabric and everything . . .'

'You're all my-mum-my-mum-my-mum,' said Ali. 'It's a bit much, isn't it? Yeah-yeah, we geddit, you've got the mum-of-the-year. Except there's NO PRIZE for making curtains. Or pancakes. Or . . .' she paused, peering at the screen. 'Are those OIL paintings of you two?'

'She's got a lot of time at home,' said Zac, defensively.

'She. Painted. You?' said Ali in disbelief. 'What's wrong with the painting phone filter? I mean, that's just, just . . .'

Tulip kicked her. 'Lovely,' she said. 'That's just lovely.' She mouthed at Ali, away from the screen, 'Be NICE.'

'Everyone's always telling me that,' complained Ali. 'When are people gonna start being nice to me?'

'We ARE nice,' protested Zac. 'We've spent all night doing research for you.'

'Yeah,' said Jay, smugly. 'To put it in your words, we've proved our hypothesis.'

'A bit of digging into the Life of Brian,' said Zac. 'Spoiler alert, there's a twist where the villain ISN'T who he says he is.

Ali and Tulip looked at each other. They knew what was coming.

'Look,' said Jay seriously. 'Don't wanna freak you guys out, but we haven't been messaging you non-stop for an hour just for funsies. Whoever he is, that creepy guy who's living with you, he *isn't* the respected Professor Brian Sturgeon. And we can prove it.'

'Well, go on,' said Tulip, calmly. But she reached out for Ali's hand. Squeezed it. 'You've got our attention.'

'For a start,' said Zac, 'Sturgeon's parents aren't dead. So when his mate Mr Plaice calls home to the mothership and chats to his folks in the village, that lie's gonna unravel real quick. They're still in the local golf club.'

'Well, that's a really mean thing for him to say,' agreed Ali. 'Killing off his parents to avoid a boring conversation about them. But that's not PROOF.'

'And Sturgeon disappeared to an off the grid

Pacific island to study the effect of some mad disease on the brain. Caused by eating animal brains or something. Tribal tradition.'

'We know that too,' said Tulip. 'He came back. Worse luck. Probably caught his case of insane-in-the-brain out there.'

'But what if he never came back?' said Jay. 'He went away this perfectly nice-but-nutty brain-doc with ginger hair and a tattoo, and came back looking different, acting mean, not knowing his own parents' names, and basically behaving like someone else altogether.'

'Well, I guess people can change,' said Tulip, doubtfully.

'But what if . . .' said Zac, 'some other guy, some NO ONE, decided he wanted Sturgeon's life? His money, his reputation? Because Sturgeon's the right pigeon to pick for identity theft. He's away on some island without Wi-Fi or data. He wouldn't even know.'

'But his friends?' argued Ali. 'Family?'

'He avoided them all, remember,' said Tulip. 'Some NO ONE, huh? What guy would want that guy's life?'

'And date Mum,' said Ali. 'Don't forget that bit. What guy would turn up out of the blue, claim he's some seriously rich neurosurgeon, and then want into OUR family?'

'Nan-Nan said that she didn't get why *anyone* would date Mum with baggage like us, because we're basically wolverines,' said Tulip.

'And Nan-Nan went off with that photo,' mused Ali. 'It's not here, anyway.'

'What photo?' asked Zac.

'There was a break in, and some ginger cat burglar was ransacking Sturgeon's place— gave us an excuse to go through all his room-rubbish . . .' said Ali, without drawing a breath.

'And we found one of Mum's old school photos in a book,' said Tulip, 'and Nan-Nan was looking at it all weird. It had a shot of this geek-creep-kid.'

'Yeah,' said Ali, 'some curtains-for-hair Science-fraud who crushed on Mum when she was like thirteen.'

'Called Evelyn!' said Tulip, trying not to giggle. 'Poor kid. Parents so keen to mess him up. Evil-in!'

'A boy called Evelyn?' asked Jay. Then he shrugged. 'Makes Wiggie sound OK.'

'Evelyn!' laughed Ali, 'Oh Evelyn, Evil-In-And-Out!'

There was a noise from upstairs. The girls stopped, they hadn't realized they'd been talking so loud. And then they heard heavy steps coming down the stairs. The kitchen door swung open, and there was Sturgeon. He was holding his cup of tea. And looking really confused.

'What's going on?' he said, looking madly around, like there was someone hidden behind the counter or under the table. 'I thought I heard someone calling . . . my . . . I mean, who's here, what's going on?'

Tulip said sweetly, 'We're study-buddying with the Other Twins. Got a project . . .'

'My name,' said Sturgeon. 'Did you say my name? Thought I heard someone . . . calling, laughing, *mocking* . . .' His eyes went a bit wild. He saw them staring, and rammed his shades back on.

'We might have said Sturgeon a few times, Sir,' called out Zac from the screen. 'We're doing a project on over-fishing in the Atlantic.'

'And we weren't mocking at all, Sir,' added Jay. 'They're deadly serious things. Fish.'

'Creepy things don't even have eyelids,' pointed out Ali.

'But not as creepy as the big businesses doing the over-fishing,' said Tulip. 'We were just saying they're Evil-in . . .' she paused, watching Sturgeon's eyes go so wide his shades wobbled weirdly over his eyebrows. 'And out,' she finished. 'Evil-in-and-out.'

'Right,' said Sturgeon. 'OK. That all sounds . . .'

'Credible, *Daddy*,' said Tulip. 'It sounds credible. Plausible. The most likely diagnosis, as Mum would say.'

'Ah, yes,' said Sturgeon. 'Don't bother your mother. She was tired so she's had some medication. I offered it when she brought the tea. And I have to go out now. So be good, twins.' His eyes fell on Ali's phone, frowning at Zac and Jay. 'And twins.'

A card fell out of his jacket as he put his empty mug of tea in the sink. Tulip picked it up, helpfully.

'A tattoo parlour?' she said. 'Are you getting Betsy removed from your clavicle?'

'Ah yes,' said Sturgeon. 'Removed. Yes. And it was Betsy, you said. Definitely not Betty?'

'Definitely,' said Ali. Raising her eyebrows. 'You could always look to check?'

'Right,' said Sturgeon, 'Put yourselves to bed, then,' and he wandered out.

Zac and Jay were shocked.

'Put *yourselves* to bed?' said Jay. 'How would that even work? Who does the night-night songs and the cuddle-tucks?' Ali rolled her eyes at Tulip.

'His parenting skills suck so hard,' said Zac, with un-Zac-like crossness.

The boys clearly couldn't understand why the girls were high-fiving, with a fist-bump-and-pump, pulling away with wavy fingers.

'Were you guys in a different conversation to the one we just saw?' said Zac, confused.

'They don't get it,' said Ali, in delight. 'Yay, my favourite thing in the world is telling other people how clever I've been!'

'*We've* been,' said Tulip, running to the window. 'Let's wait until we're sure he's gone.'

She ran to the window. And watched Sturgeon striding away up the street, followed by Witch, who was leaping at his pockets again. He was ineffectively swatting her away.

'Hahaha,' cackled Tulip. 'Hey Ali, your Ali-cat's been well-trained.'

Ali came to the window too. She saw a

movement in the shadows. And a slim figure began running athletically down the street. Keeping to the wall.

'Did you see that?' she said to Tulip.

'I did,' said Tulip. 'Your powers of observation are improving.'

'I can't improve,' said Ali stubbornly. 'I'm PURRfect, remember.'

The figure stayed in the shadows, avoiding the streetlights, but then a car drove up the road. She was briefly illuminated, along with Witch's eyes.

They saw a woman in black, with a fedora hat, a mop of wild red hair spilling under the brim.

'Ginger!' the girls said in unison.

'She's tailing Sturgeon,' said Ali.

'But she totalled his office?' said Tulip.

'Guessing she didn't find what she was looking for.'

'A-hem,' said Jay, 'I'm gonna regret this, but why were you guys so pleased with yourselves?'

'You were righ . . . righ . . .' said Ali. 'Nope can't say it. Too hard.'

'You were right!' said Tulip. 'He IS an imposter. We've got a great idea who he is. Or rather, who he was.'

'Well, who is he?' asked Zac, reasonably.

Tulip looked at Ali, who nodded significantly. 'Let's say it in creepy-twin-unison! Drumroll, dum-dum-duh!'

'Evil-in-Sprotland!' they said together.

CHAPTER 20:
THE OTHER MUM

But at that moment, there was a noise behind the boys. Their door had been opened. Their curtains swished shut. The boys turned around.

'Sorry, Mum,' said Zac.

'Yeah,' said Jay. 'We'll be down in a moment.'

'What are we doing?' repeated Zac to his mum. 'Oh, just chatting to the Other Twins. Give us two minutes.'

'What do you mean the Other Twins,' bristled Ali. 'You're the Other Twins! You're the . . . Twinferiors!'

'No, you are,' said Jay.

'No, you are,' said Ali.

'No, YOU ARE!' Ali and Jay yelled together, crossly. 'Jinx! Aargh!'

'Tell us tomorrow,' said Zac, sensibly. 'All About Evelyn. Mum's told us to put our phones downstairs before the bedtime story.'

'And she's finally got to the good chapter in the Lord of the Rings,' said Jay.

'Literally had four hundred pages of hobbits walking and talking to get to this bit,' agreed Zac.

'What!' said Ali. 'What about OUR big reveal!'

'Can't wait!' said Zac. 'See y'all tomorrow at the Fayre.'

'Boys!' the other twins' mum came back into the room. She had a bright headscarf that she was hastily tying on, 'Sorry, girls,' she said. 'It's no-screen time before bed. See you at the Fayre. Say hi to Minnie. Night, night.' And she clicked off the call firmly.

'Oh-that's-not-on,' said Ali, crossly. She threw her own phone so it skidded across the room, and ended up under the sofa.

'Don't think I'm getting that for you,' said Tulip.

'Shouldn't have let them in our team,' grouched Ali. 'Ditching us for some lame hobbit story just because their gluten-free-curtain-making-home-baking-oil-painting-stay-at-home says so.'

'Well, it's bedtime,' said Tulip, reasonably.

'And what's with that headscarf . . .' said Ali, 'Who wears one at home?'

Tulip sighed, and patted the sofa. 'Ali-bear,' she said. 'You know how we're being doctor detectives . . .'

'Duh,' said Ali. 'Is it Obvious-Day?'

'Well,' Tulip carried on carefully, 'aren't there a bunch of medical mystery clues about Zac and Jay's mum?'

'Like what?' said Ali, 'The scarf she's started wearing? Even indoors. Like Stupid Sturgeon and his shades.'

'No, *not* like Stupid Sturgeon,' said Tulip. 'So, she's suddenly at home a lot. Doing arty-bakey stuff for the boys. Like she's on a break from her work.'

'And . . .' said Ali.

'And, Zac said she'd not been well . . .'

'You said that, already,' said Ali. 'I thought he was talking about OUR mum and got mixed up . . .'

'Teensy bit self-centred, that,' said Tulip. 'And you mentioned the scarf? She's just started wearing a scarf over her hair . . . like all the time.'

'Hiding a bad hair job,' suggested Ali, tentatively, as she finally got what Tulip was saying, and didn't want to admit it.

'Must have been a *really* bad hair job,' said Tulip, ''cause it got her eyebrows as well.'

Ali didn't say anything. She counted silently off on her fingers all the things that Tulip had said. Zac said she'd been ill. She'd become a stay-at-home. She'd hidden her hair.

She finally spoke, in a small voice, 'She's not hiding her hair. She's *lost* her hair. All her hair . . .'

Tulip nodded. 'I think that's why Wiggie shaved off his hair, too,' she said. 'I think she's had . . .'

'Chemo,' said Ali, finishing her sentence. 'Chemotherapy. She's got the Big C.'

They both knew what the Big C was, from when they were little, and Mum would come back from the cancer ward, sometimes just quiet and sad, and sometimes a bit tearful.

And Tulip and Ali would ask, 'Did you lose one today?' without really thinking what that meant.

Zac and Jay's mum was one of those ones.

'I said she was a sad-stay-at-home,' said Ali. 'I think I'm feeling that thing when you feel bad for what you did or said.'

'Guilt?' suggested Tulip.

'Or maybe just that I'm sorry I said it,' said Ali, a bit more bullishly. 'I mean it's not like I KNEW. I'm just thinking that maybe I shouldn't have . . .'

'Regret?' suggested Tulip. 'It's nice you're building your vocabulary.'

'Hmm,' said Ali. 'Their mum painted them an OIL PAINTING. That's like a real . . . memory-building, forever thing.'

'Don't beat yourself up,' said Tulip.

'I made fun of it,' said Ali. 'I'm such a noob.'

'Hey, you're *our* noob,' said Tulip. 'But you solved the mystery of the other mum. So maybe you'll be nicer about her now.'

'I'll be really nice to her at the Fayre,' promised Ali. 'I'll even eat her gross gluten-free-egg-free-cupcakes.'

'They won't be gross,' said Tulip. 'They'll be delicious. She puts caramel popcorn on them.' She got up and started going up the stairs. 'I'm gonna check on Mum.'

Ali followed her, 'She should be checking on us,' she complained.

Mum was half-asleep, already. 'Mum,' said Ali, a bit crossly. 'What did stupid Sturgeon GIVE you? You haven't even had dinner yet. There's some gross goat's cheese thing downstairs that's got your name on it.'

Mum yawned, and stretched out on top of her duvet. 'You're not really selling it to me, munchkin,' she said. 'Brian found my commute-fruit and chocolate. He gave it to me when I came up. So I've had that. But now I'm just SO SO tired . . . and this horrible, bobbly rash . . .' She'd pulled a sock over her arm up to her elbow, to stop herself scratching.

'Mum,' said Tulip, seriously. 'Sturgeon's drugged your chocolates. And he's not who he says he is . . .'

'Yeah, I'm locking the door on him,' said Ali.

'Oh munchkins,' said Mum mildly, not really taking it in. 'I'm sorry he's not who you thought he'd be. I was hoping he'd be good for you.'

'Mama-bear,' said Tulip, tentatively. 'Does Sturgeon remind you of someone you used to know? Nan-Nan told us about this kid who used to hang around. When you were at school. Evil-In-Sprotland.'

'Poor Evelyn,' murmured Mum. 'So awkward. He was a bit chubby. Chubbier than me, I mean, and he had this really big hair, just to hide behind . . . he was so devastated about that last science project thing, he made such a scene when he got found out.'

Mum turned over, like she was already asleep. Ali had to nudge her to keep talking. 'What scene?' she said.

'Oh, they said he'd never be a scientist. Something silly like that. And he said he'd show them all,' said Mum. 'And then he cried. I told him he could be whoever he wanted. He emailed me when he left the school. Said I was the only smart person in the school, the only nice one, too . . .'

'Were you nice to him?' asked Tulip.

'Of course,' said Mum. 'I'm nice to everyone. You know, it's nice to be important, but it's . . .'

'Important to be nice, blah-blah-blah,' said Ali. 'I know, you've got it stitched on a heart-shaped cushion somewhere.'

'You ever thought, maybe, that Sturgeon's a little bit like Sprotland?' asked Tulip.

'Not a bit,' said Mum, rolling over in bed. 'Evelyn ate for England and had massive hair. Brian never touches a carb if he can help it. Not even milk in his tea. Keeps his hair super-short . . .'

'Weirdo,' sniffed Ali. 'Seriously, Mum, why'd you ever date him?'

'I'm not sure,' said Mum, yawning. Her voice was hardly more than a whisper. 'He seemed really certain that it was a great idea. He suggested it over coffee, after our first box of chocolates together. I ate them all.'

Mum stretched out like the Witch-cat, and she was sound asleep.

'I guess,' said Ali, 'that whatever he gave her, it makes her really suggestible.'

'Seriously dodgy drugs,' said Tulip. 'Probably combined with a bit of cheap hypnotism.'

'I'm locking him out,' said Ali, and she kissed Mum carefully, and tucked the duvet over her. 'Sleep tight, Mama-bear, we'll sort out the super-villain.'

Downstairs, Ali double-locked the door, and dragged a table against it. Piled up chairs against the back door. She crouched under the sofa, and dragged out her phone, and called Nan-Nan.

'Girls?' said Nan-Nan, immediately. 'What's up?'

'We're not letting Sturgeon back in the house,' said Tulip, bluntly. 'He's just given Mum more drugged chocolate.'

'Don't worry about Sturgeon,' said Nan-Nan. 'Got eyes on him. He went to some tattoo place, and now he's heading to his country house. I'm betting he's staying there tonight.'

'Where are you?' asked Tulip. Nan-Nan sounded breathless, like her phone was bouncing. 'Are you exercising again?'

'Yes, yes,' said Nan-Nan testily. 'That's it. Dancercising.' They could hear traffic noise. A siren. 'Gotta go,' she whispered. 'Fayre, tomorrow. I'll have people there!'

The phone went dead.

'She'll have people?' said Tulip. 'What people? Like the guys who run the lucky dip?'

'And she deffo wasn't at home,' said Ali. 'Poor, confused Nan-Nan. I forget she's getting on a bit. Because she's so Nan-Nan all the time.'

The girls locked the windows.

Brushed their teeth.

Put on pyjamas.

Unlike Zac and Jay, they knew how to put themselves to bed.

But instead of going to their room, Ali went to Mum's.

'What?' she said, defensively. 'I'm just checking she's OK.'

'All night?' said Tulip.

'Yeah, maybe,' admitted Ali. 'What if . . . I don't know, she went into cardiac arrest. Or pulled off her itch-mitten.' She curled up in the bed next to Mum.

'Sometimes I forget you're still little,' said Tulip. 'Because you're so YOU all the time.'

'Are you coming?' asked Ali, making a space.

''Course I am,' said Tulip, 'but I'm bringing Twoo!' She went to get her new owl.

The girls cuddled up, one on each side of Mum, like guardians at a door.

'Seriously, stuffed toys,' sniffed Ali.

'I brought the spare alpaca for you,' said Tulip. 'This one didn't get chucked into the enclosure.'

'Well give it here, then,' said Ali, and she cuddled it contentedly. 'Ha!' she muttered. 'You called him *Daddy*. More than once.'

'Yeah,' said Tulip. 'It worked and everything. Still feel like I need a shower.'

CHAPTER 21:
FAYRE ANGELS

The next morning, there was no Sturgeon. No news from Nan-Nan. And Mum was back to being droopy-headed.

'What were you playing?' she asked, drowsily, stumbling around the house to see all the doors barricaded. 'Forts or something.'

'Or something,' agreed Tulip. 'Are you sure you wanna go to the Fayre, today?'

'The Fayre?' said Mum, and her head lifted suddenly. Like it was some sort of trigger phrase. 'Yes-I-have-to-go,' she said in a strange monotone. She shook her head, and spoke in her normal voice. 'You wanted me to go, right?'

'You sounded weird, just then,' said Ali. 'You heard that, right?' she asked Tulip.

Mum shrugged, 'Oh, munchkin, everything's weird with you. Brian's weird, Nan-Nan's cooking's weird, the other twins are weird . . .'

'All of those ARE weird,' pointed out Ali, 'kinda proving my point.'

'Do you really want to go to the Fayre?' insisted Tulip.

'Yes-I-have-to-go,' said Mum, in the same robo-monotone. Before sipping her coffee and asking brightly, 'Are you OK just with cereal, munchkins? There'll be cakes at the Fayre.'

'Yeah, I heard the weird too,' said Tulip in a low voice.

They dressed in the clothes that were closest to the top of the pile dumped on the floor. Mum hadn't been paying much attention to their room-tidying lately. Ali gave a cursory sniff-test to her purple leggings.

'Honestly,' said Tulip, 'What are you expecting them to smell of?'

'These were the ones I used to smuggle the chocolate bars upstairs,' said Ali. She tossed them aside, and pulled on another pair. And then put shorts over the top. And then put a short T-shirt on top of her long T-shirt.

'You always double-dress,' commented Tulip, pulling on jeans and a T-shirt. 'Bit unnecessary.'

'Totes necessary,' argued Ali. 'Means I can always lose a layer if I need to. If a maniac grabbed my T-shirt, or a crazed cat got me by the shorts, I could literally just rip them off.'

'Well, you can always hope,' said Tulip, grinning. 'Shame to waste your prep.'

She frowned at her reflection in her phone, and tied up her hair in tight bunches that stuck out on each side of her head.

'I'm not going out with you like that,' said Ali. 'Add a cuddly toy and you look like the annoying cutesie baby sister in literally any cartoon ever made.'

'Hair's too long,' said Tulip briefly, 'It's over my ears.' She picked up the scissors from her desk, scattered with coloured paper and stickers, and decisively cut off both the bunches, just above the elastic. She tossed them into a plastic bowl, filled with her hair tufts, like mini-shaving brushes.

'Now that's unnecessary,' said Ali, blowing up her fringe. She'd left it so long it was falling over her eyes.

As they left the house, Mum absent-mindedly petted Witch, who was sitting on their wall, now. It seemed she'd given up on the vet's, now Mum put out milk for her.

'She's sweet,' said Mum, as Witch purred and stretched luxuriously. 'It's nice she likes Brian. Most cats attack him. No idea why.'

'Instinct?' suggested Tulip.

'Taste?' said Ali.

'Doubt it,' said Tulip. 'No self-respecting cat would taste *Brian* if he was served up with fish sauce.'

'Girls,' said Mum, mildly, as they started the short walk to school. 'Be nice . . .'

When they got in, the Fayre was busy, but lots more people looked zombie-zonked out. They fitted right in with Mum. Like they were sleepwalking.

'It's spreading,' hissed Ali to Tulip. 'Busy Brian. He must've got more of them than we thought!'

'School's fault for letting him do that stupid study,' said Tulip.

'Oh look,' said Mum, 'The other twins are there! Their mum makes the BEST cakes.'

Jay and Zac were with Mrs Khan and their parents. Their mum was painting the backdrops to some stall, finishing a complicated-looking design. She was wearing another bright scarf on her head, and paint-spattered overalls.

'Hello girls,' said Wiggie, waving them over to join them. 'Would you be fair angels and help the boys deliver these cakes to the stands? Someone's been baking all night.'

'Fair angels!' said Ali, bristling. 'That's wrong on so many levels! Fair? Angel? You wouldn't call the BOYS fair angels.'

Jay coughed. And then Zac turned around apologetically. They were wearing matching rainbow T-shirts.

With the legend *Fayre Angels* written in a bouncy bubble script.

'OMG,' said Tulip, 'Matching T-shirts? That's so, so . . .' She recovered, as Ali was choking with suppressed laughter into her sleeve. 'So . . . supportive!'

'Yeah,' said Jay, bluntly. '*We're* the Fayre Angels. We deliver cakes and tell the parents where the loos are and stuff like that.' He looked coldly at Zac. 'HE volunteered. And I . . .' He shook his head in disgust. 'Got dragged under the bus.'

'I think you both look adorbs,' said Ali, sniggering. 'Well-jel!'

'Well, we can't leave you out of the fun,' said Mrs Khan, still yawning. She pulled out another pair of T-shirts from the box. 'Pop these on, girls. That way everyone knows you're official and not just stealing the donated cakes.' She looked at their mum a bit too hard.

'What?' said Mum. 'Why are you looking at me...' She trailed off. 'Ooh, those do look yummy,' she said, spotting the cookie stall. 'Happy helping girls! See you laters, alligators...'

'Poor woman,' said Mrs Khan, shaking her head. 'It's like an addiction.'

'Well, let's spread these little lumps of joy around,' said Ali, shrugging on the shirt.

'Thank you, Ali. And you too, Tulip, that's really kind of you to help,' the other twins' mum said. The girls looked at each other. They were surprised she knew their names. They didn't know hers.

'Oh, no worries,' said Tulip, taking the first tray. 'Happy to do our bit.' She noticed that the cupcakes were cut into quarters. 'Are these all free samples?'

'That's the idea,' said Mrs Khan. 'On every stand, please. That way everyone gets a bit of free cake.'

'Why are they so purple?' asked Tulip.

'They're lavender, dear,' said Mrs Khan. 'It's a very NOW recipe, apparently.'

They walked off with the boys. 'That's funny,' said Ali. 'Nan-Nan made lavender cupcakes yesterday. Smelt like wardrobes.'

'I think they smell more of hand cream,' said Zac.

'You use lavender hand cream?' asked Ali.

'We're not cavemen,' said Jay. 'Of course we do. Don't you?'

Ali surprised him by taking his hand in both of hers. 'Feel how soft my hands are?' she said sweetly. 'That's because I don't use paper to wipe my bottom. I just go cavegirl and USE MY HANDS . . .'

'Eee-urgh!' choked Jay, jumping away. 'You're so gross.'

They stepped carefully over a tantrumming toddler pounding the ground, while her harried parent tried to reason with her. 'I'm walking away,' said the dad drowsily. 'I'm gonna walk away . . .'

'He's so not gonna walk away,' said Tulip, and the dad returned, and tried to pick up the child, who screeched and arched her back. And yelled I-hate-you-I-hate-you. The tired dad sighed and put her back down again.

'Free cupcake, Sir?' said Jay helpfully.

'Oh, thanks,' said the dad, accepting it. He ate it and seemed to perk up immediately. He shook his head and opened his eyes wide. 'I know someone who likes tickles!' he said to the toddler, tickling her tummy. She screeched again, but this time with laughter, and crawled on his back. The dad picked her up and bounced jauntily away.

'Wow, what's in the cakes?' said Zac. 'Must be something herbal.'

'Never mind the cakes,' said Tulip. 'We're gonna tell you our big reveal.'

'Let's walk then talk,' said Jay. 'Need to dump these on every stall.'

It took them a while to drop off all the cakes. People seemed to love them. The Fayre was getting a lot more noisy and jolly, so they stopped at a quiet spot near the back of the school. The grumpy too-tall kids were hanging out there on their bikes, shirtless and smoking. Pulling show-off wheelies.

'Check this out,' said Ali, and she showed them Mum's class photo on her phone. 'Found this same shot in Sturgeon's office.'

'So he nicked a pic of your Mum?' said Zac. 'That's weird.'

'Mum still had her pic,' said Tulip. 'Turns out, wasn't HER class picture. It was HIS.'

'WHAT!' said Jay, staring at the shot. 'You mean, Sturgeon was at school with your mum?'

'And really liked her, according to Nan-Nan,' said Ali. 'She was the only person who was nice to him.'

'But . . .' said Zac, staring at the shot, 'well, he's not there, is he?'

'We didn't get it straight away, either,' said Tulip. She zoomed in on the shot of the moon-faced kid staring through his curtains of hair.

'I'm no artist like your mum,' she said modestly, 'but check this out.' She coloured in the kid's specs, so they were dark, like Sturgeon's shades. Scribbled a hat on him.

'Now just imagine him without cakes or carbs at all, because Sturgeon won't touch them. And super-short hair.'

'Seriously, that's so mad,' said Zac, staring at the shot. 'Who was he?'

'Introducing Evelyn Sprotland,' said Ali. 'Evil-In-Sprot-Land. Poor kid didn't have a chance with a name like that.'

'Nominative determinism,' said Jay wisely, 'Like Sturgeon said in the hospital café. If that's what you're called, that's what you'll be.'

'Like Bore-Boy?' asked Ali innocently.

'Like Ali-cat,' snapped Jay.

'I win,' said Ali. 'I've got claws.'

'Hey, you! Fayre fairies,' yelled one of the shirtless boys. 'Get-outta-here. This is our place.'

'We're TALKING,' yelled Ali back to them. 'Haven't you got some empty cans to kick around a park playground? Bus stop to mooch about? Shopkeepers to terrorize?'

'You're pretty mouthy for a foetus,' scoffed the kid.

'Spell foetus!' challenged Ali.

The kid looked furious. 'F-E- . . .'

'Wrong,' said Ali, with satisfaction.

'We're just talking,' said Jay. 'And I'm going to report you for smoking on school property,' he added, recklessly. The big kid approached him, and he backed away. Into the weedy bushes at the edge of playground. Tears started running down Jay's face.

'You crying?' laughed the kid, in a mean way.

'I AM NOT,' said Jay, offended, pushing back his glasses. 'I have allergies. And urticaria.'

'Ha!' said the kid. 'I can't beat up on a baby girl. But I can bash you to bits, Brainiac.'

'*He's* not the Brainiac, Jerk-face,' complained Ali. 'He's just a hypochondriac. And no one bullies my besties apart from me,' and she ran up and kicked the big kid hard in the shin.

'Ouch!' said the kid, shocked. Like he'd never been hit before. He seemed a little scared of Ali. She hissed and held out her nails like claws. His friends went to grab her, but she just wriggled fiercely, and her Fayre Angel T-shirt came off, so she could slip away from them.

'See,' she told Tulip triumphantly. 'Double-dressing works.'

'Where's Zac?' asked Tulip, looking around. She hadn't noticed Zac disappear, but he was already wandering back with Mrs Khan, who was munching on a cake. She was looking much more lively, too.

'You!' she shouted. 'And you! All of you! Off school property!'

The boys spat out their cigarettes, and casually slouched off, wheeling their bikes. One of them dropped his shorts at the gate, showing his bum.

'Joke's on you,' yelled Ali. 'We don't lip read!'

Mrs Khan turned to her, shocked. Her mouth started to tremble. She wasn't cross. She was holding in a laugh.

'Carry on, girls,' she said, nodding. And she strolled back towards the Fayre.

'How'd you do that?' said Tulip to Zac. 'You literally disappeared, and no one spotted you.'

'Easy,' shrugged Zac. 'I just took off the rainbow shirt. You were looking out for the uniform.'

'OMG,' said Tulip, waving the photo of Evelyn Sprotland. 'What if Sturgeon's here? Just not in HIS uniform.'

'I was looking out for a guy with hat and shades,' admitted Ali.

'Mum!' said Tulip desperately, staring into the crowds. 'Find Mum! We can't let him get to her.'

They raced around the Fayre. Everyone was scoffing the free lavender cakes like they tasted nice, or something.

And then Tulip saw something mad. She saw Mum. Walking with a super-strange-speedy march like she had at the hospital. Mum was heading up to a group of children with something in her hand. A flash of a needle.

Just like she had in the lab.

'Muuuuuum!' yelled Tulip. 'Nooooooo.'

CHAPTER 22:
THE RETURN OF GINGER

Ali's head snapped around and she saw what Tulip saw. They ran towards Mum in what felt like endless-slow-motion screaming. Mum just kept going relentlessly towards the children.

But then, a black and ginger flash overtook them.

Someone was running faster than them, a slim woman in a black trench coat, with a fedora hat jammed over bright ginger curls.

'Ginger!' yelled Ali and Tulip.

'Who?' said Jay and Zac, who'd been running after them.

'That's the cat burglar,' said Tulip, drawing to a halt, clutching a stitch. She bent over painfully.

'She's not a cat burglar,' said Mrs Khan, who'd marched over towards them. 'She's a patron. She donated all those cakes for the Fayre.'

'What!' said Ali. 'You gave everyone sweets from a stranger? You never heard of Stranger Danger? What if they were drugged, or something.'

'Whatever they are, they're delicious,' said Mrs Khan, taking another cake.

'Forget the cakes,' said Tulip. 'We gotta stop Mum!'

But Ginger had got there first. She jumped on Mum and knocked her to the ground, wrestling the thing out of her hand and smashing it to bits. Then she grabbed Mum's shoulder bag.

'Hold on,' said Ali. 'Mum didn't have that shoulder bag when we left.'

'Well, who gave it to her?' said Tulip.

'Didn't Sturgeon have that bag at the zoo yesterday?' said Jay.

And then Ali saw him.

No hat. No shades. Short hair. Shorts. He looked like anyone else.

'Take *that* everyone else's powers of observation!' yelled Ali triumphantly. 'Look!' She pointed him out. 'Check that guy.'

'What guy?' said Jay, squinting in the distance.

'That NO ONE guy,' said Ali. 'Imagine him chubby with curtains for hair.'

'Evelyn Sprotland!' said Tulip.

Everyone else ran forward to help Mum, when Ginger leapt on her. He was the only one backing swiftly away.

'Evelyn Sprotland?' repeated Zac and Jay in chorus.

The man's head jerked. He'd heard the name. He looked around wildly.

He saw Ali and Tulip and Zac and Jay pointing at him in the crowd.

He saw Ginger standing over Mum, and dusting herself off. She'd carefully rolled a jacket under Mum's head.

And then he backed away again. Faster and faster.

And then he started running.

Ali and Tulip looked helplessly between Mum and the man.

'Mum?' said Tulip. 'We gotta help Mum!'

'We've got her,' said Zac. 'You get him!'

'Really?' said Ali.

'Really,' said Jay. 'We're a team. Remember.'

'You mean *Unfortunately*!' said Ali. And she began running.

'Great way to say thank you, bestie,' yelled Jay.

Ali raced determinedly after Sprotland-Sturgeon. And Tulip, after a moment's hesitation, followed.

'Get the school nurse,' Tulip yelled over her shoulder.

'On it!' called Zac. Nurse Han was already heading over to Mum with her white box.

The girls were chasing after him, and then it happened again. The ginger woman overtook them, running with inhuman speed. She bounced a couple of metres between strides.

'Hey, quit that!' yelled Ali. 'Stop showing us up!'

The woman just laughed over her shoulder, and gave them a little wave bye-bye.

'I can't believe that Sturgeon's so fit,' complained Ali, out of breath.

'He ran a lot,' said Tulip. 'Probably had to work really hard to keep the fat off. In case someone recognized him as chubby Sprotland.'

'That's why the poor sucker hated cake in the house,' said Ali. 'Couldn't even have milk in his tea. Almost feel sorry for him.'

Ginger was calling someone on her phone; it

flashed from her trench coat. And then there were sirens, as police cars came bearing down from all directions. They'd just got to the bridge that crossed the wide river into town. Sturgeon was in the middle. Trapped. There were police cars on either side.

Ginger was approaching.

And then he started climbing the tall metal mast at the middle of the bridge.

And climbing.

Climbing higher. Like a crazed King Kong in his shorts, which flapped against his skinny legs in the wind.

'Oh,' said Tulip. 'So . . . that's . . . unexpected.'

CHAPTER 23:
PLOP GOES THE WEASEL

Ginger did something strange. She turned, and beckoned them over.

The girls looked at each other warily, and approached.

'Come on, munchkins,' she said crisply. 'Spit-spot, I haven't got all day. Let's do this thing.'

'Nan-Nan!' squealed the girls. 'What are you doing here! You're Ginger!'

'Now girls,' chided Nan-Nan, pushing back the bright curls from her face. 'That's a little bigoted. We prefer Red-headed.'

'But you can WALK!' said Ali. 'You can RUN!'

'And how,' said Nan-Nan, lifting her trousers. Underneath were metal legs, with a blade-like limb sliding into her trainers. They looked strangely familiar.

'Your legs!' said Tulip. 'Those were the twin sculptures in your basement! You said they were out of use!'

'Well, they get pretty sore,' said Nan-Nan. 'Better off than on. Unless strictly necessary.'

They walked towards Sturgeon, who was dangling above the swirling river. He didn't look too safe up there.

'How were the cakes?' asked Nan-Nan, looking at the girls.

'Didn't have them,' said Ali. 'They were *herbal*. And purple.'

'I meant, how were they working?' said Nan-Nan, rolling her eyes. 'I got the girls in the lab to do a bit of experimenting with the lab rats. We used the poison that Sturgeon had been stabbing in people. Made the rats nap, unsurprisingly. Got a nasty rash, too. And then we used a bit of this stuff, that you found in the shoebox, to see what would happen.'

She pulled out the tube from her pocket. From the stash that they'd stolen from Sturgeon's room. It was labelled ADT, with a dot that had been struck through.

'Do you like riddles, girls? This one was easy.'

'Dot,' said Tulip. 'But it's been erased. No-dot? Un-dot? Anti-dot?'

She looked at Ali, and it dawned on them at the same time. 'Anti-DOTE!'

'Please stop saying things at the same time,' said Nan-Nan. 'It creeps out the normals.'

'They *were* working,' said Tulip. 'Everyone was eating cake. And getting a lot less sleepy. Mrs Khan even threw out the biker kids.'

'Good-good,' said Nan-Nan, walking briskly. 'The rats woke up too. Started exercising, actually. Like they'd stored up their energy.'

Nan-Nan and the girls stopped under the spot where Sturgeon was clinging.

'Well, well,' she said pleasantly. 'Your dastardly plan failed. So we can do this the easy way or the hard way?'

'Who ARE you!' shouted Sturgeon. 'You've ruined everything! Why did you do that! Why!'

'Why did I stop you poisoning a school?' asked Nan-Nan. 'If you've gotta ask the question, I think you're the one who needs a doctor. Maybe you'd better come down, dear.'

'I was poisoning them to CURE them!' yelled Sturgeon. 'I was going to be a HERO. And finally get the glory I deserved in Year 9! I was going to create and cure Sturgeon's Sleeping Sickness!'

'Hey, you were right,' said Ali, nudging Tulip. 'You said he was such a rubbish doctor, he needed to make people sick so he could get the credit for making them better.'

'Munchausen by proxy,' said Tulip wisely. 'Knew I was right. Just didn't want to gloat.'

'Except you're *not* Brian Sturgeon,' said Nan-Nan.

'I AM SO,' said Sturgeon wildly. 'I can prove it!' He tore open his shirt dramatically, and showed a tattoo on his collarbone. Betsy. It looked a bit raw and red. Like it was brand new.

'You see,' he said triumphantly. 'Only Sturgeon has this tattoo. No one else knows about it! Hahahahaha!' His laugh was demented.

'Except that the tattoo was on the other side,' said Ali, bluntly.

'What!' said Sturgeon.

'Didn't you know?' said Tulip. 'That's what Plaice said in the café. You should work on your listening skills.'

'The other side?' shrieked Sturgeon. 'The OTHER side!'

They heard someone call behind them. It was Mum, riding in Momo's taxi. He waved happily to the girls, honking the horn. Mum climbed out and ran towards them on the bridge.

'Munchkins!' she said, hugging them. 'And Mama-bear! Thanks for jumping me in the playground. Loving the hair! What are you doing here?'

'Cleaning up your mess, dear,' said Nan-Nan. 'It's kinda my job.'

'Not this time,' said Mum, and she took a decisive bite out of the cupcake that she was carrying with her.

'Brian,' she called up. 'I've just realized that I've no idea why I'm dating you. I don't even like you. Sorry about that.'

'Catch up, dear,' said Nan-Nan. 'He's not Brian Sturgeon. He's that weird Sprotland kid who used to try and impress you with his stolen science projects.'

'Evelyn Sprotland?' said Mum, frowning as she looked up at him.

'They were NOT stolen,' shouted Evelyn. 'Minnie, you were the only one who believed in me. Said I could be anyone I wanted to be! And I proved you right! I made myself the most impressive doctor in the WORLD.'

'What?' said Mum. 'Evelyn? What have you done? Did you drug me, or hypnotize me, or something?'

'So you could help me!' said Evelyn. 'So we could collaborate! Share the Nobel! I did it for you!'

'Oh,' said Mum, 'Well, that's . . .'

'Gallant! Dashing! Extraordinary!' said Evelyn, a touch too hopefully.

'I was going to say a little bit sick,' said Mum. 'Anyway Brian, I mean Evelyn. No hard feelings. Enjoy prison. Or the psych ward. I won't be visiting you, obviously . . .'

And with that, Mum turned around. 'See you later, munchkins,' she said to the twins, as she bounced energetically on her toes, 'I'm in the parents' 100 metres race for the best cake in the world back at the Fayre. The other twins' mum made it. And it's got my name on it.'

'That was awesome, Mum,' said Tulip. 'You're back.'

Mum grinned, and waved goodbye.

'Noooo,' called Sturgeon. 'Minnie, please! I did it for you!'

Someone fainted in the bustling crowd. The police started shouting for a doctor. 'Oh well,' said Mum. 'Back to the day job. I'll get cake later.' And she jogged over briskly to help.

Sturgeon was still calling out to her piteously. Weeping.

'It's over, Evelyn,' said Nan-Nan, almost kindly. 'In every possible way. Identity-theft. Stealing. Poisoning . . . the list goes on. What did you think was going to happen when the real Sturgeon came back from the Pacific island where he's been working . . .'

'He was never going to come back,' said Sturgeon with gritted teeth. 'I'd have made sure of that . . .' He realized what he'd said, and backtracked hastily, 'Or something less incriminating, I mean . . .'

'So let's add plotting murder to the list,' said Nan-Nan. 'Now get down, dear. You're wasting our time. Minnie will resuscitate that person back there in a moment, and you know how she inhales cake, she won't leave us any.'

'Never!' howled Sturgeon, swinging from the high bit of the bridge. 'You'll never take me . . .'

and he pulled out a syringe, with a wild light in his eyes. '. . . Awake!' And he stabbed himself in his skinny thigh. Again and again. Using up the whole dose. A bubbling rash appeared around the area, and he fell asleep instantly. His other hand began to loosen from the metal bar where he'd been clinging.

'Yuck,' said Ali, looking at his legs, with the pus-filled spots breaking. 'Pop goes the measle.'

His hand finally let go. And Sturgeon was falling down towards the slow-flowing river. Snoring as he whooshed passed them. He made a hole in the water where he landed.

'And plop goes the weasel!' added Ali, triumphantly.

'Oh,' said Tulip, hanging down to look at where he'd fallen. 'That was unexpected, too.'

'He can swim, right?' said Ali.

'Well, I'm not getting wet,' said Nan-Nan. 'The wig's expensive. And my metal legs might rust.' A river-rescue speedboat was rushing towards where Sturgeon had fallen. Two rescue divers were already in the water.

'Think we've done our bit,' said Nan-Nan, decisively.

They turned and walked off the bridge, and

Nan-Nan gave her report to a police inspector, before sitting down in the wheelchair that a police car had brought for her. She twisted off her legs, with satisfaction.

'Gross,' said Ali. 'Can I try those on, sometime?'

Nan-Nan just laughed, as she propped her legs down the side of the chair. 'Was it really meant to be on the other clavicle?' she asked. 'The Betsy tattoo.'

Ali shrugged, and looked at Tulip, who smiled sweetly. 'What are we, medics?' she said.

CHAPTER 24:
UNLESS STRICTLY NECESSARY

'Why do we have to have a service for Stupid Sturgeon?' complained Ali.

'Well, Mum thought it was a nice thing to do,' said Tulip. 'They haven't found him yet.'

'And he'd already bought a funeral plot behind my house,' said Nan-Nan. 'Probably planning to hide the real Sturgeon there, if he ever came back. Might as well make use of it and dump his stuff there.'

'Weird having a funeral without a body,' said Ali.

'We've got his body of work,' said Nan-Nan. 'Means you can have your playroom back.'

At the cemetery, Mum had brought Sturgeon's

stuff in boxes, and they buried them in his plot. Zac and Jay's parents had turned up too. With home-made snacks.

'Poor old Evelyn,' said Mum, happily munching. Back to her old pre-Sturgeon self. 'He really was quite psychotic.'

'You're lucky you got away from him,' said Wiggie. 'Your girls were amazing. They were the ones who exposed him.'

'And not just his collarbone,' said a tall woman, standing behind Ali and Tulip. She was wearing a fedora low on her face, and a long black trench coat. She had a mad wig of steel-coloured curls.

'Who are you?' said Ali. 'You his mum, or something?'

'No, I am not,' said the woman, with superb condescension.

'You're dressed like Ginger,' said Tulip.

'Yes, I am,' said the woman. 'But my name is Silver. I work with your Nan-Nan. In, the, you know . . .' She stooped and whispered, 'S.W.A.T. team.'

'Senior Water Aerobics Training team?' said Tulip.

Silver nodded. Significantly.

'Your work is sterling,' said Silver, in a low

voice, 'Detective work. Medical work. We've assessed the underground video of you in action. The blog. The police report. We are *impressed*, girls. I have a proposition . . . there's a medical mystery, that you might just be able to help with . . .'

Nan-Nan saw them talking, and rolled over crossly, 'What are you up to, Silver?' she whispered. 'This is possibly the most inappropriate place you could rock up. It's a funeral!'

'For paperwork, Ruby,' scoffed Silver. 'Excuse me if I don't pay my respects.' She looked seriously at Nan-Nan. 'You must know, Ruby, with your long years of service, that we would avoid using children unless it was strictly necessary . . .'

Nan-Nan leaned back. 'OK, Silver,' she said. 'You've got our attention. What's the job?'

The girls stared between the two of them, wide-eyed.

Back at their house, Mum ushered the other twins up the path, while Wiggie and his wife waved to them from their car.

'Thanks for watching the boys, Minnie,' he called. 'We're off on our date night!'

'What's a date night for your folks?' said Ali grumpily to the boys. 'Polishing their halos? Running a soup kitchen?'

'Think they're going to a pottery class,' said Zac. 'Mum sells her ceramics for charity.'

'For charity?' said Ali, aware of how Ali-catty she sounded, but it was too late to take it back.

'Yes, charity,' said Jay. 'It's not all about looking after us, you know. Mum does have a life.'

'How lovely,' said Nan-Nan, rolling into the front garden, 'My little cookie-crumbles! I said we'd have your little friends around for a tea party!'

'Hah!' said Ali. 'Forgot you did that. Not your finest hour.'

'I know your finest hour,' said Jay, with a grin. 'You stood up for me. You said I was your bestie.'

'Aaargh!' said Ali. 'Shut up, I hate you, shut up.' She paused at the doorway. Turned back impatiently. 'Well, come on, then. There's cake. And 12 rated movies.' Jay grinned and followed her in.

Tulip and Zac stood outside for a moment. 'What WAS your superpower?' she asked. 'Being invisible? Being a good liar?'

'Both of the above,' said Zac. 'Actually, I like to think I help make people better. You know, like my bro. And my mum.'

'Like a doctor?' asked Tulip.

'Not like a doctor,' said Zac. 'Just, you know. Like to look after people.'

He grinned at her. 'I'm so glad your mum's better.'

Tulip thought that was big of him. 'Cause his mum wasn't better. Yet. Maybe she would be. It was too early to tell.

'Aww. Thanks,' said Tulip, following him in.

Witch sat stiffly on their wall. Looking annoyed. Hissed at the closed door.

With comic timing, Tulip opened the door again. 'Well, come on, Witchy,' she said. 'It wouldn't be a party without you.'

Witch gave her a dignified look, which said *I knew that.* Casually licked her paws, like she wasn't in a hurry. And with a satisfied Me-Wow she stalked into the house like she owned it.

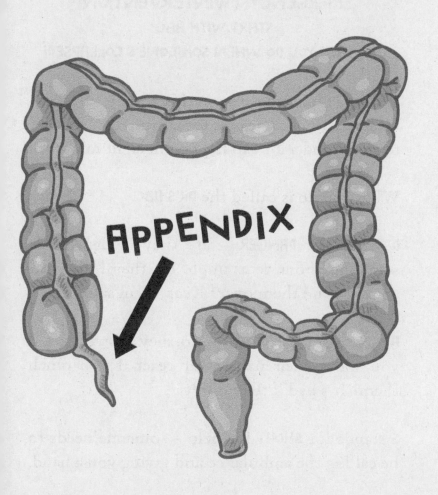

APPENDIX

Tulip says: An appendix is an extra bit at the end of a book. It is also an extra bit dangling off your gut.

EMERGENCY TWINTERVENTION!
START WITH ABC
OR WHAT YOU DO WHEN SOMEONE'S COLLAPSED!

Well, you have to do something, right? Because it can take eight minutes for an ambulance to get to them, and a lot can happen in eight minutes.

What you do is called the **DR'S ABC**.

D stands for **DANGER** – are they in danger? Is someone about to trample on them? Is a car about to run them over? Keep them safe!

R stands for **RESPONSE** – do they answer you if you shout their name? Or react if you pinch them? It's bad if they don't.

S stands for **SHOUT** for help - someone needs to be calling the ambulance and giving you a hand.

A stands for **AIRWAY** - check if it's blocked. They might be choking on something. Or it could be swollen if they've got an allergy and ate peanuts in their curry.

B stands for **BREATHING** – if they can't, you might need to breathe for them. Basically that means holding their nose and breathing through their mouth to inflate their lungs. It's gross but it could save their life until someone gets there with a special mask to pump air into their lungs.

C stands for **CIRCULATION** – if their heart isn't pumping the blood round to their organs, they're in trouble. You might need to do chest compressions to pump the blood around.

D E F G is **DON'T EVER FORGET GLUCOSE!** Sometimes people collapse because they've had a hypo, which means they don't have enough sugar in their system. So if you know that's what the problem is, give them some!

PS. My sister says this blog is lame but I know she's cross she didn't think of it first.

COMMENTS: WED 8.45 A.M.
OMG TULIP CHECK OUT THIS ON YOUTUBE, IT'S LIKE THESE TWO KIDS ON THE TUBE READ YOUR ABC BLOG! ZAC 😱😦
PS HOPE YOUR CAT IS OK.

TWINTERMISSION!
TOILET TALK
OR WHAT DOES YOUR POO SAY ABOUT YOU!

We all like a bit of toilet humour. But when you do a funny poo, so funny it could have its own cha show, like Ali says, that's deadly serious. You migh not notice your own poo—it's flushed away an forgotten. But it tells you a lot about your health.

That's why someone invented:

THE BRISTOL STOOL CHART .

If you're not pooing at all, or pooing dry hard bit (Type 1), you might need to drink more, eat mor vegetables, that sort of thing.

If you're pooing a squirty mess (Type 7), you'v got a bug, and probably best not to eat anythin more than dry toast and apple purée, to give you gut a break.

Basically, what you want is big, nicely-formed wet, easy-to-pass sausage poo, like Type 3 or 4. I your poo is on the gross ends of the chart, go and see your GP!

(But don't hang out round a hospital if you've go Type 7 diarrhoea, as you're probably infectious, and you'll make all the sick people worse . . .)

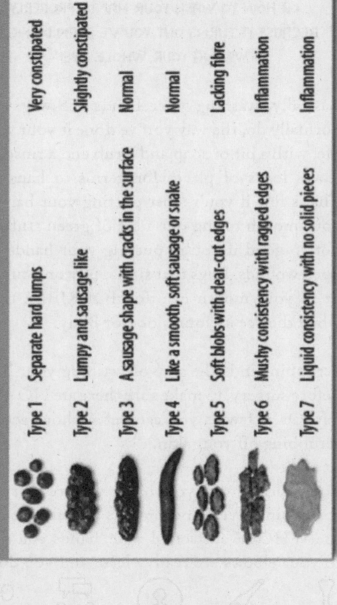

BRISTOL STOOL CHART

Type 1	Separate hard lumps	Very constipated
Type 2	Lumpy and sausage like	Slightly constipated
Type 3	A sausage shape with cracks in the surface	Normal
Type 4	Like a smooth, soft sausage or snake	Normal
Type 5	Soft blobs with clear-cut edges	Lacking fibre
Type 6	Mushy consistency with ragged edges	Inflammation
Type 7	Liquid consistency with no solid pieces	Inflammation

TWINTERMISSION!
SCRUBBING IN
OR HOW TO WASH YOUR HANDS PROPERLY
BECAUSE IT TURNS OUT YOU'VE BEEN DOING IT
WRONG YOUR WHOLE LIFE!

Basically, washing your hands the way you'd normally do, the way you've done it your whole life, with a bit of soap and a rub and a rinse, still leaves loads of places for germs to hang out. That's fine if you're just putting your hands in your mouth to tug out a bit of green stuff, but not so good if you're putting your hands near open wounds. Bugs that sit happily on your skin or in your mouth can do HORRIBLE things when they're in your blood or body.

Scrubbing in is the way of washing your hands before surgery, to make sure there are NO germs left. Or as few as you can get without actually scrubbing off your skin.

You basically wash your hands with really strong soap doing special movements to make sure that the WHOLE surface of your hands and down to your elbows are really clean, and you do it a few times, and it takes about five minutes. Once you're clean, you can only touch sterile things, like the inside of a surgeon's gown, before you get your gloves on.

HERE'S HOW YOU SCRUB IN.

Lots of soap that you pump with your ELBOW not your hands

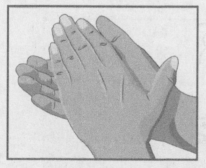

1) Palm to palm, rub-rub-rub, a few times.

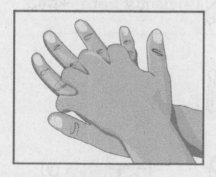

2) Each hand over the back of the other hand, ditto with the rub-rub-rub, etc.

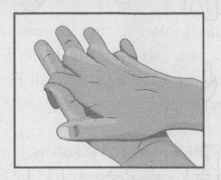

3) Fingers interlaced.

4) Clasp hands, both ways.

5) Round the thumb.

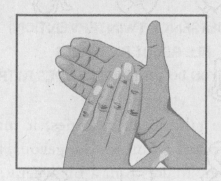

6) Nails in the centre of
each palm a few times and all
the way down to the elbow.

AND START AGAIN,

do all that twice more

AND THEN

you can put on sterile stuff.

EMERGENCY TWINTERVENTiON!
ALL ABOUT ALLERGIES
OR WHAT YOU DO WHEN ALLERGIES ATTACK!

When people talk about allergies, it might be something irritating but not dangerous, like Mr Ofu's hayfever. Makes him a bit weepy, sniffy, and itchy, but won't kill him. A nice antihistamine usually sorts out the allergic reaction.

My friend Jay's got urticaria, and he gets big itchy weals (raised red patches) on his skin, and itchy eyes, when he's around HIS allergens, pollen and animal fluff. Really not nice, but anti-allergy meds will calm it down. The red patches can disappear in a few hours, so lots of people turn up to the doctor the day after and have nothing to show them. So take a picture when you've got the reaction, it'll help your GP make the diagnosis. Then you'll be prepped with the right meds for the next time it happens.

The worst allergic reaction is ANAPHYLAXIS! That's when you react so badly that your body stops working how it should, your throat might close up with swelling, so you can't breathe, and your blood won't go round well enough to make your organs work. It might be caused by a bee sting, a bit of peanut, something really small that you haven't even noticed.

That's when you need your EPIPEN (if you have one)—just stab it into your thigh. And if you don't, get to A&E, and they'll give you all the meds within MINUTES. Basically adrenaline, steroids, and antihistamines.

COMMENTS : SAT 9.53A.M.
AWESOME ON ALLERGIES, TULIP! BUT COULD YOU PLEASE DELETE THE BIT ABOUT MY URTICARIA!

ADMIN: SAT 9.55A.M.
AWW, YOU READ MY BLOG? 😊 HOW ABOUT I JUST USE YOUR INITIAL, TO KEEP YOU ANONYMOUS. MY FRIEND J. INSTEAD OF MY FRIEND JAY.

COMMENTS: SAT 9.57A.M.
YOU'RE KIDDING, RIGHT? SAY IT OUT LOUD. HOW IS J DIFFERENT FROM JAY? DELETE IT!

ADMIN:
OH, GOTCHA. OK. 👍👍

COMMENTS:
AND YOU KNOW MY URTICARIA IS MEDICALLY CONFIDENTIAL INFO, ANY STUFF A DOCTOR KNOWS ABOUT YOU IS MEANT TO BE PRIVATE, WHY DON'T YOU WRITE A BLOG ABOUT THAT!

ADMIN:
GREAT IDEA! CAN I INTERVIEW YOU FOR IT?

COMMENTS:
UM, OK. BUT DON'T USE MY NAME.

ADMIN:
SURE, ALI SAID SHE'S GOT LOADS OF GREAT NAMES TO CALL YOU INSTEAD. COME OVER. ZAC TOO.

COMMENTS:
HAHAHAHAHA. WE'RE ON OUR WAY. JAY AND ZAC

Thank you for visiting
the Mini-Medix Blog.
Come again!
#MiniMedix

ACKNOWLEDGEMENTS

Thanks to everyone at Oxford University Press, especially lovely Liz Cross, for not judging me about my double doughnut habit and for making writing this book so fun. Thanks to wonderful Catherine Pellegrino at Marjacq, for believing that I could write for children. Thanks to the superwomen of James Street Writers - Clare Morgan, Alice Jolly, Jacqui Lofthouse - for reading my early drafts.

Thank you to my patients, and the staff in the hospitals who have hosted my rotations, in Surgery (of all sorts, from brains to big toes), Intensive Care, Anaesthetics, Emergency, General Practice, Oncology, Dermatology, Cardiology, Neurology and more. You are heroes. You teach me something every day.

And my biggest thank you is to my family and friends, for all the love and support. Especially our kids, my closest and most critical readers—Alia, Zarena, Zaki and Jaan—who listen to all my books out loud at bedtime, and tell me firmly when something could be better. They outnumber me so I have to listen to them...

ABOUT THE AUTHOR

Roopa Farooki is a junior doctor working for the NHS in London and Kent. She has four children (twin girls and two boys).

Roopa is also the award-winning author of six literary novels for adults, that have been published in over twenty countries, and has been listed for the Women's Prize for Fiction three times. She received an Arts Council Award and Author's Foundation Prize for work that increases understanding between cultures. She lectures in creative writing at the University of Oxford, is a Royal Literary Fund Fellow and is the Ambassador for Family for the relationship charity, Relate.

She says that doctors, detectives and writers have something in common, they all like to solve mysteries, and work out what makes people tick.

@RoopaFarooki

Here are some other stories we think you'll love...

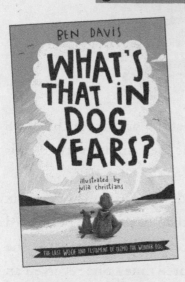